The Bitter Pill

Mike Forsyth

© 2019 Mike Forsyth. All rights reserved
ISBN 978-0-244-75413-6

Acknowledgements

My sincerest thanks go to Mrs Helen Parker for her advice on publishing and to Peter, The Old Man of Storr, for his advice on the area of Knoydart, Scotland. I would also like to thank my two daughters, Tabatha and Betsy, for keeping the book a secret.

This book is dedicated to my Lieb. Without her love, support, advice and guidance, it would not have been possible.

Prologue

She rested her head against his chest and stroked his cheek with her slender hand. For that moment the carnage of the previous forty eight hours had disappeared and the only distraction was the first birdsong of the morning, briefly offering hope of bright new things. His eyes had not moved from her for some time, even while she slept. His first thoughts upon her rousing were of her utter beauty, her fragility and how he wanted to protect her. At that moment he did not know whether he was protecting her from a malevolent force that had swept through the brief time they had spent with each other, or whether he was protecting her from herself. She rubbed her eyes with the back of her hand, smudging her eye make-up even more than it had been already. The pillow she had laid on was smeared with henna and rouge, whilst her hair was still perfectly curled on the left side but flattened slightly on the right where she had laid on it after succumbing to exhaustion.

This was the first time he had seen her in her natural state; without the bright lights, the perfect make up, the perfectly set blonde hair. To him she was even more beautiful because of it. She looked up to meet his gaze and smiled, exposing a flash of her teeth and the creases to the side of her eyes that had had barely three hours rest. He cradled her face and looked into her blue eyes. "I'd die for you," he said, his eyes fixed to hers.

"Why on earth would you want to do that?" she said, her voice croaking due to her dry mouth and her sparkle disappearing to be replaced with an expression more representative of the circumstances in which they found themselves.

"Because," he said, pausing to kiss her on the forehead, "some things are worth dying for."

Chapter One

Robert Johnson glanced up at the clock on the wall of the office, and to his relief it was five to five. He slouched back in his chair and watched as one of his cohabiters leant over his desk, their furious scribing being the only sound which deviated from the clock ticking away like a metronome. Personal effects were not permitted on desks, save for a tea cup, as they served as a distraction to work. The walls which surrounded him were filled with shelves full of dusty ledgers dating back decades, whilst the view from the window behind his desk was of the neighbouring factories and offered little distraction on the rare occasion that Robert bothered to glance out of them.

His office was shared with two of his colleagues. Arthur Treadwell was, Robert assumed, in his late fifties, although he had never had this verified. Arthur had worked at Simpsons Ltd, a factory which made glass bottles, since he was fifteen. He had married his wife when he was nineteen after they had been childhood sweethearts, their lives together only interrupted for four years in 1914, when Arthur had fought for his country in the First World War. He was not decorated, he was not a recognised hero for any acts of valour or bravery, but he had fought and survived and returned home to his wife and his job and had worked his way up to be Financial Accountant of Simpsons Ltd by the age of thirty two. He had stayed in this role ever since, and one of his duties was to manage the work of Robert. He was once a slim man, and sporty, having represented the local village cricket team, but now led a mostly sedentary life. His stomach portrayed the signs of his desk bound job, of being well fed by Mrs Treadwell and of his love of emptying some of the bottles produced by Simpsons for the local brewery into it.

The second person who shared the fifteen by twelve foot grey-walled room was James Thomsett, who had joined the company aged fifteen and had risen to the ranks of sales ledger clerk. James was a bright young spark who dreamt of replacing Arthur Treadwell one day. He was engaged to be married to his sweetheart, Eileen, and was saving for a life with her, putting all of his spare money aside to be able to afford a ring for her finger and the rent for some rooms locally. James was too young to have fought in the war, but asked Arthur often about life in the trenches and hung off his every word. Robert had heard the stories multiple times, and groaned inwardly every time they were recounted. He did not care to be reminded of his own experiences; of what he left behind and of what he returned to. But he respectfully allowed Arthur his right to tell his stories of death, destruction, disease and dysentery; although quite why he wanted to was beyond Robert.

It was clear to Robert that Arthur saw James as his natural successor. He was motivated, focused and single-minded, but most importantly listened intently to his every word and acted meticulously on every instruction. He was everything that Robert used to be when he first started at Simpsons in 1918, seventeen years previously. Incrementally this had been chipped away at until he had been left simply going through the motions. He turned up for work at nine am sharp, he stayed until five pm, and he worked diligently during that time, but his motivation, his care, his passion for progression had long since gone. As the clock hit five o'clock exactly, Robert closed his ledger for the day, picked up his jacket and hat from the stand that stood next to the door, and opened the door to leave. "You not coming, Jim?" he said to his junior counterpart.

"Just want to stay and get this work finished, Robert. Arthur's expecting it by Thursday."

"Well that's alright then, it's Tuesday, you silly sod. He's not back from the Board meeting yet anyway, and he's in with the General Manager first thing tomorrow morning. That gives you plenty of time to get it done. Come on, come and have a beer at The Bell" Robert said, swallowing at the thought of the first pint of Porter.

"No I can't" James said, regretfully.

"Course you can, if you can get the work done tonight then you've got time to do it tomorrow, haven't you?" Robert said, doing his best to cajole his young colleague into offering him the chance of some company as he drank.

"It's not just that, mate. You know how I'm fixed with money. I need to put everything aside to get myself some rooms for me and my Eileen." At that Robert was relieved that the obstacle was merely financial.

"Come on, Jim. I'll get you a couple of beers."

"A couple!" exclaimed James, aghast at the thought. "If my Eileen smells beer on my breath my life won't be worth living. She'll think I'm squandering our opportunity of a life together" the young clerk replied, clearly showing that he had had the same conversation with his betrothed many times before.

A short walk later, the pair sat ensconced in the corner of the pub. James took a sip of porter and licked his lips with satisfaction. "Cheers, Robert, you're a diamond. I can't remember the last beer I had."

"I know the feeling", Robert replied, lying, as he took a deep hit of the strong black coloured nectar. It punched the back of his throat and instantly settled him. Robert was not what one might consider the classic definition of an alcoholic. He managed to maintain his life and his job, pay his bills, just, and if he had any relationships, they would not be suffering as a result of his drinking, he was sure of that. But he drank on a daily basis, not to excess so that he was ill or unable to get up the next morning, but often. He drank to nullify the tedium of his existence, of what he had lost, and of what he longed for. Whilst his young companion cradled his beer, talking of his plans for his life and his future happiness, Robert finished his Porter and made his way to the bar for a second, which was closely followed by a third and a fourth. At some point between the fourth and fifth, James had offered his apologies and had returned to his family home where his chop and boiled potatoes were being kept warm for him by his mother. This, despite the company and distraction that James offered him, was of relief to Robert, who examined what was now left in his wallet and scraped together enough shrapnel to afford himself what would be his last pint until he was paid on the Friday. For the next two evenings he would have to rely on what remained of a bottle of rum to provide the same comfort that he gained from the locally produced porter. He would not be returning to a warm chop, or a warm embrace, but would have to settle for stale bread and butter to soak up the alcohol, before retiring to his bed alone.

Robert was born in the winter of 1899 after a long labour which his mother had not survived. His father was a respected man of self-made wealth from a string of prudent ventures. This had afforded him the opportunity to keep Robert at the distance which he felt necessary after the death of his wife. Robert had a nanny between his birth and his fifth year, upon which he was sent to boarding school near the Kent coast, where he would stay until he would bring sufficient enough shame to his father to give him reason to sever all ties with him. The coldness he had become accustomed to had shaped his youth and made him insular. He had no real friends at school to speak of and had focused instead of studying hard to try and emulate his father's achievements. He had enlisted at fifteen and survived the war to return to lodgings paid two months in advance by his father, and a one off payment of £100. A parting gift which would serve as a foundation to build on so as not to heap the shame of poverty on to his father on top of what he had already blighted him with. The £100 was gone within the year, wasted on alcohol and poor business decisions.

He had married by the early spring of 1919, to the first girl who showed any interest in him. Elizabeth was pretty, polite and respectable and Robert endeavoured to build a life with her, to have children, to have a warm family home, full of love; everything that he had been denied. Once married, however, it became clear that Elizabeth was cold, was not maternal, and wanted merely the financial security that marriage to Robert could offer. Or so she thought; the poor girl clearly had not realised that Robert had no significant security, and no chance of any without the financial backing of his father. Their marriage became loveless very quickly, although in truth it always had been, with Robert simply craving a family and Elizabeth merely stability. The bed they shared soon became sexless and subsequently the home they shared remained childless. Elizabeth died of pneumonia in 1927, leaving Robert widowed aged twenty eight. He mourned her, as a friend, but she had never been a wife to him and as such he had avoided repeating the same mistake by marrying again. He had even less to offer than he did previously anyhow, so remained single and chose to avoid the company of women by and large, barring the odd drunken dalliance after last orders. These encounters served merely to satisfy his animal urges, infrequently, as opposed to being any great quest for love. Now, aged thirty six, Robert found himself alone, in a job he hated, with no future that he could envisage.

Sitting alone in his favourite pub, he surveyed his surroundings as he made the most of his drink. The sight was of laughter and merriment, of jokes being told, of men clamouring for the attentions at the bar of the new barmaid, both for drinks as well as for something far more satisfying. She would clearly be an asset to the landlord, her winks and smiles and the way she sashayed from one end of the bar to the other ensured plenty of activity. It was no coincidence that the bottles of Timothy Taylor, kept on the bottom shelf opposite the bar, had suddenly become the most popular selling drink, with anyone ordering them being guaranteed a good view of her behind as she bent down to retrieve them. After finishing his porter and warming his hands on the heat generated by the crackling fire, he left the Bell and began his walk home. Despite the recent fine weather, the temperature had turned for the worse and a storm brewed menacingly above him. He pulled his jacket around his chest in an attempt to retain the heat that he had enjoyed at the public house, but to no avail, and as he reached the corner of Fisher Street the heavens opened. If his finances had allowed he would have turned and sought refuge back in the Bell, but that option was not open to him. As he trudged through the freezing rain he cursed his generosity towards Jim. But these feelings were fleeting; he liked Jim, who would no doubt have the life that Robert had once hoped for himself. Within a few minutes he had reached home, having run the final few hundred yards in a vain attempt to avoid saturating his only suit.

Upon entering his modest lodgings, he picked up his mail, glanced at a letter which appeared to originate from Scotland and immediately discarded it on the sideboard, before pouring himself a tot of rum. He stood and sank his first rum, knowing he should eat and go to bed. Any more alcohol would make him feel ill in the morning, but he poured himself another drink. He sat and stared into the room, his wet arms resting on the worn surfaces of the solitary chair. The sparseness of the room was in stark contrast to the vibrant hustle and bustle of where he had spent the earlier part of his evening, as was the silence. He had become accustomed to his own company, with scant reminder of the past limited to a photo of Elizabeth on the sideboard and some trinkets that adorned the mantelpiece whose significance and meaning he had long since forgotten. His mind wandered to the new barmaid at The Bell and he pictured her stood naked in front of him, smiling, eyes sparkling and with her hair tousled because of the rain. He could do with her being there in reality; although in truth he would not have had a clue where to start with her. It had been months since he had been with a woman and cheeky patter was not really his forte. He sighed and finished his drink, then wandered over to the sideboard to get another one. He opened the bottle and went to pour, but his eyes were drawn to the letter he had previously ignored. Mail to his address usually signified requests for payment or notification of an increase to his rent, either way any mail was as unwelcome to him as the prospect of work in the morning was. But the postmark intrigued him, and his interest got the better of him. He put the bottle back down and ripped at the envelope clumsily, tearing part of the letter inside in the process. He opened the letter up and did his best to focus on what he was reading, with difficulty due to both the volume of the alcohol that he had already consumed as well as the lack of food.

"Dear Mr Johnson,

You are invited to Manor House, Knoydart, Scotland, for the reading of the will of the late Thomas Deacon...."

He froze at the sight of the name that he had not seen written or heard spoken of in years, but that had been so instrumental in how his life had evolved from privileged son of a self-made millionaire entrepreneur to mid-thirties accountant wearing dead men's shoes for a bottle factory. He continued reading;......"please find enclosed a train ticket dated Friday September 13th on the 10.00 Royal Scot train from Euston to Glasgow Central, where you will be met and taken to Knoydart. Please be prompt and bring sufficient and suitable clothing for the weekend. The matter will be of advantage to you."

"Friday 13th," he muttered to himself. "That's this Friday. Suitable clothing…..what the hell does that mean? Suitable for what, exactly? And why the hell has Thomas Deacon requested I attend the reading of his will after everything that had happened between us?" Robert went straight for the rum and poured himself a large measure then sat back into his armchair, still wet from the rain, still staring into the exiguously populated room, mind still wandering. On this occasion, however, it was not a naked barmaid stood in front of him. This time it was Thomas Deacon.

Chapter Two

Sir Roderick Baldwin's School for Boys had been founded in 1574, by the eponymous Tudor knight in the town of Deal in Kent, to make education available to boys of a certain standing. A great deal had changed over the centuries, but by 1914 the original building still stood and had been complimented by additional buildings adjacent to it in the mid Victorian era in order to cater for the rise in admissions. The school had originally been used by the wealthiest families in the local area, but after two and a half centuries, its reputation and success meant that the school was expanded to incorporate boarding lodges to facilitate an influx of boys from all over the country. It was a small room in one of these lodges that Robert Johnson had called home since he was five years old.

Robert had spent the ten years at Sir Roderick Baldwin's in relative solitude, although he shared his room with another boy; Thomas Deacon.

Thomas Deacon, not dissimilarly to a lot of the other pupils, came from a family with a tradition of attending Baldwin's. However, the significant difference was that the school was only still in existence because of the Deacons. Whilst it had always had an excellent reputation, like many Elizabethan institutions in the Victorian era it had begun to fall into obscurity. There was not enough local demand to keep the school financially viable, so whilst the expansion to increase admissions was partly driven by its successful reputation, it was also, to all intents and purposes, a business venture to ensure the future of the school. This had been driven by Bernard Deacon, Thomas's great, great grandfather; a local landed gentry whose vast wealth had recently been bolstered by capitalising on the Industrial revolution in terms of investment in ship building and subsequently brewing in West Kent. By the 1830s, Bernard Deacon was one of the wealthiest men in the country, and as an alumni of Baldwin's himself, had a keen interest in securing the future of the school, of ensuring his legacy lived on in the school, and of course of generating additional income for himself.

Over the next decade, his vast fortune had bankrolled the construction of a larger school to compliment the original building, four boarding lodges, a gymnasium and a dining hall, whilst he had also donated land opposite the school which became a dedicated sports field with a small pavilion. Whilst the finance required in order to build the education and boarding elements of the venture came in the form of a loan, payable over thirty years with interest at a reasonable rate, the sports field and pavilion was a gift. Such philanthropic gestures were rare from Bernard Deacon, but he was a keen cricketer and wanted to promote the game at the school. Because of the improvement in infrastructure, of facilities and the ability to attract students from far and wide the School's future was secured and would be in the Deacon's debt for longer than a mere thirty years. Facilitating this expansion ensured that the Deacon's name would forever be synonymous with Baldwin's, thus appeared Deacon Hall, the Deacon Sports Field and Deacon House along with School House, Cinque Ports House and Baldwin House now that numbers permitted dividing the school into sections. This also meant that each House could battle over the Deacon Cup, an annual cricket competition which had grown to be the pinnacle of the school year for anyone with even half an interest in sport. It was also no coincidence that every Deacon boy at Baldwin's ever since had been head boy, as well as captaining their house rugby and cricket teams regardless of talent.

By 1914, Thomas Deacon, like his father and grandfather before him, was now head boy and captain of Deacon House cricket team, despite the fact that there were older and more suitable candidates for both roles. With the role and the name also came the inevitable behaviour of invincibility. Boys queued up to carry favour with him to avoid a beating; masters were unable to punish his tardiness or poor class work; the brightest students were bullied into doing his evening work. The effect of Deacon in that tiny room ensured that Robert's senior years at Baldwin's were as unpalatable as they could be. To make matters worse, Deacon was a handsome young man. He had hair so blonde it was almost white, with piercing light blue eyes, a good complexion, strong cheek bones and the confidence needed to charm the local young ladies in the town. He was always sneaking out of school in the evening while others ensured his work was done, returning later to regale

Robert with tales of what he had been up to with the daughter of the landlord of the local pub, or the daughters of the local farmers. Robert lost count of the amount of different girls that Deacon had on the end of his string at any one time. Whilst Deacon went into lurid details of his conquests, Robert lay awake dreaming of a wife, of children, of a home brimming with love, warmth and hope. Although that, of course, was for the future, his present was focused on academic achievement as well as sporting. His build was not made for rugby, with the autumn and winter months spent mostly trying to avoid the pain of physical impact from far greater specimens than him. It was during the spring and summer months where he came into his own, excelling on the cricket pitch, where his height, speed and athleticism had made him into a menacingly accurate fast bowler. It was this that had enabled him to be the first fourteen year old to captain his house, Cinque Ports, cricket team. The kudos was so great that his father planned to travel from their family home in South London to watch him in the final of the inter-house cup against Deacon House.

Thomas Deacon was a poor cricketer. Deacon House had only narrowly beat Baldwin House in the semi-final and Deacon played little part in the success, yet to hear him that evening the victory was all down to him. His smugness made Robert's blood boil and despite trying to ignore him, it was impossible not to be drawn in when the celebratory reliving of the Deacon House win soon evolved into baiting Robert regarding the following week's final. "You've got no chance next week, Johnson. No chance. Not with me bowling at you" Deacon spat, sneering at Robert all the while.

"And what's more" he continued, "you'd better watch your back from now on. I don't want you getting any ideas above your station about bowling me out, you understand?" Deacon bellowed, his chin twitching in rage. Robert ignored him and continued trying to get to sleep, it was already late and he would inevitably have to contend with Deacon waking him up later after returning from another late night excursion into town. Deacon was not interested in letting the matter go though. "Don't ignore me you little shit! Who are you anyway? You don't belong here. Your Dad's a commoner from London, that grubby little city full of shit washed up from the Thames. You hear me, Johnson? You best bowl some crap to me next week otherwise I'll smash your face in" he snarled.

At that Deacon left for another visit to town, while Robert lay in silence until he had drifted off to sleep, undisturbed until the early hours when Deacon once again returned with breath reeking of watered down beer and tales of fumbling around with a girl called Jean round the back of the bins of the Kings Arms. The poor girl had been promised jewellery, romance and a future, in return for her compliance. She had kept her side of the bargain, by all accounts. Deacon scoffed at her naivety in expecting him to keep his side. Robert despised him.

The proceeding days followed a similar pattern of direct threats then disturbed sleep thanks to Deacon's debauchery, until the night before the final when Deacon resolved to have an early night to ensure he was fresh to punish Robert's "dog shit bowling", as he termed it.

"Charming", Robert thought to himself. As he closed his eyes and thought about bowling Deacon out first ball, over and over again and celebrating, fists clenched and grinning wildly.

The following day, lessons finished early so that everyone could get over to the field and get on with the main event. In no time, the players were changed and ready and the masters and parents were seated as comfortably as one could be in the wooden chairs that sparsely populated the boundary, whilst the non-participating students sat cross-legged on the grass. The weather was fair and the conditions perfect, as Deacon and Robert strode out to the middle with the two umpires for the toss. The Headmaster, Mr Clarke, who was umpiring from one end, took a coin from his pocket and flipped it in the air. "Your call, Deacon" the Head instructed, as Robert rolled his eyes at the predictability of Deacon getting to call.

"Heads" he boomed, confidently. The coin landed on tails.

"Your choice, Johnson" Mr Clarke said, much to Deacon's displeasure.

"Best of three, surely" said Deacon, desperate to gain any advantage. But Mr Clarke was having none of it, surprisingly.

Robert opted to bat first; turning to his team mates and tapping his leg to let them know to start getting their pads on, whilst Deacon warned, "Just remember what I said, Johnson, you little shit," his eyes fixed on Robert with a steely stare.

As Robert walked back to the pavilion to join his team mates, he looked at the boundary's edge, looking for his father. The boundary was heavily populated, being mandatory for all pupils and masters to attend; whilst the parents had turned out in their dozens to see their children participate. He could not see him, which was not a shock to him despite his letter confirming his attendance which had arrived the previous morning. However as he neared the edge of the pitch, he then spotted his father walking up the gravelled path towards the field. It had been the first time he had seen him since the Easter weekend, the previous time being Christmas, with all contact seeming to revolve around the holidays. This was the first time his Father had visited him during term time since he started at Baldwin's in 1904, such was the honour of captaining your house cricket team. Despite the distance between him and his father, both geographical and emotional, Robert had always endeavoured to make him proud. His appearance had filled him with a burning pride in his chest, which very quickly turned to fear and panic at the thought of letting him down.

The game got underway and Cinque Ports made a healthy start and had scored eighty four runs for the loss of three wickets by the time lunch was served. Lunch was a light affair consisting of sandwiches with a variety of fillings, cold meats, salads and tea. Whilst the majority tucked in heartily, Robert felt sick at the thought of food due to nerves as well as the uncomfortable atmosphere at having to speak with his father. Although pupils were sat separately to parents inside, on the way to the hall, his father had sought him out and told him he was proud of Robert. Those words had never been uttered to him before and had both unsettled him and delighted him in equal measures. He felt accepted at last; he felt he had pleased his father. He resolved to do his utmost to win the Deacon trophy. It still prevented him from eating anything though; he just sat with his team, looking at his father talking to other parents, whilst Deacon's father looked to be in fervent discussion with the headmaster. The headmaster was a man to be feared; tall, barrel-chested, with a moustache that looked like a paint brush that had been dipped in bright white paint. Any boy who had the misfortune of being sent to him always returned having been soundly caned. Robert had never been on the wrong end of the cane, but had heard talks of Mr Clarke making a hop, skip and a jump before delivering the first of many blows. He had been at Baldwin's for years and had even been headmaster when Deacon's father was a pupil, although one would not know it by the looks of how Deacon Snr was lecturing him during lunch.

After the interval the game continued at a pace, with wickets tumbling and runs being scored in quick time. Soon it was Robert's turn to bat with only three and a half overs remaining. There was not enough time to score anything meaningful, so he just resolved to not get out. He finished on fourteen not out and the total that Deacon House had to beat was two hundred and twenty one runs. He strode off the pitch to raucous applause from his own housemates, all neutrals who had suffered at the hands of Deacon, as well as the masters and parents, including his father who had a broad grin on his face.

Deacon House's reply, of course, would begin with Thomas Deacon and his partner, Daniel Waterfield, a much better batsman who would have to play second fiddle to Deacon who insisted on facing the first ball, which would be bowled by Robert. Robert marked out his run up and turned to face Deacon, he looked left and right, his field set and ready.

Deacon glared at him and bellowed, "remember what I said Johnson." Robert ignored the threat. He refused to be intimidated by him, and delighted at the prospect of dismissing him, especially in front of his father and Deacon's parents who watched on from the side lines. The headmaster called for play to begin and Robert began his run up, delivering a fast ball just outside the off stump. Deacon swung and missed by a mile, and the ball just missed the stumps and thudded into the wicket keeper's hands. Deacon glared at Robert, who smirked back at him. "You bloody fool, Johnson." Deacon spat with rage. Robert was unmoved by it, having been filled with a strange feeling of confidence that he normally lacked in everyday life. He was buoyed by his father's words, of his batting, and now of the prospect of humiliating Deacon. He did not care about the consequences. All that mattered was the present.

He ran in to bowl the second ball and once again, Deacon swung and missed with the ball tantalisingly close to hitting the stumps. Robert was just getting into the swing of things, a couple of loose balls and then his accuracy would kick in. He ran in for the third time and the ball arced in from the left and was on its way to hit the stumps. Deacon, eyes shut and face contorted, swung wildly and his bat just caught the edge of the ball which flew backwards over the slips and for four runs. "Ha! That showed you, Johnson. Bloody awful ball, got what it deserved." Robert smirked, which served to annoy Deacon even more. Both boys knew that Deacon was talking nonsense and that he had got lucky. The Deacon House boys all cheered ferociously, whilst the other boys cheered for Robert, clearly enjoying the sparring between the two of them. Robert ran in once again, releasing another near perfect delivery which Deacon, playing with more care, just attempted to block. The ball was far too good for him, however and caught the edge of his bat, flying in between the wicket keeper and first slip for four more runs. "And again, Johnson. You really are rubbish at this game aren't you" he bellowed, loud enough for the spectators to hear, who cheered with delighted chants of "Deacon! Deacon! Deacon!" This ruffled Robert, who feared he was not living up to the expectations bestowed on him. He walked back to the start of his run up, looked at Deacon, who stood there smugly grinning back at him, and began tearing in towards his foe.

Deacon had been boosted by his second four and returned to the tactic of wild, blind swinging, but Robert was in his stride now. His arm was warm and his accuracy perfect. The ball was delivered and swung from left to right, missing Deacon's swat with the bat and smashing into the middle stump. The crowd cheered, Robert celebrated with a cry of "Howzat?" while Deacon looked aghast.

"Not out" replied the Headmaster, steadfastly.

"What?" Robert pleaded, wheeling around to face the headmaster with horror etched into his face. "Howzat?" Robert repeated, as Deacon roared with laughter.

"I told you not out, Johnson. The Sheer impertinence to even question me!" snarled Mr Clarke.

"But…but." Robert uttered, incredulously.

"But nothing" the headmaster admonished. "It was a no ball."

"NO. No it wasn't." Robert pleaded, "I bowled him fair and square." There were gasps from the boundary, no one quite believing what was happening.

"That's your final warning, Johnson." Mr Clarke threatened, "Once more and you'll be sent off for poor sportsmanship." Robert took a deep breath and bit his tongue, pacing back with urgency. He turned to face a delighted Deacon, bolstered by the knowledge that he had been given a free pass by the headmaster. He looked to the boundary to see his father clearly unsettled by the proceedings, fidgeting in his seat, whilst Mr Deacon tutted his disapproval at Robert's outburst.

As he began his run up for the final ball of the over, Deacon hollered "try to bowl properly this time, Johnson." Robert's pace gathered with renewed vigour, his teeth gnashing as he tore up to the crease. Deacon grinned and braced himself, raising his bat slightly, ready to swing, but Robert pitched the ball far shorter than normal. The ball hit the pitch half way down the track with great pace, and as Deacon swung, the ball bounced up aggressively and caught him on the side of the temple, dropping him to the floor like a wet rag. Robert froze, as time seemed to stand still. All he remembers were his team mates rushing to see if Deacon was okay, the headmaster bawling in his face and the melee that was ensuing on the boundary's edge. The game had ended after six balls, awarded to Deacon House due to poor sportsmanship by their opponents' captain. Deacon would spend the next three weeks in a coma; Robert was suspended from school and his father would never speak to him again.

Before a disciplinary panel had an opportunity to meet to decide his future, the country had been plunged into a war with Germany and the Austro-Hungarian Empire and fifteen year old Robert Johnson was on his way to France to fight for his country.

Chapter Three

A loud blast from a horn startled Robert back into reality as he ambled across Arundal Street towards Simpsons Factory, his mind awash with over twenty years of history that had led him to where he was now. The last two days had been filled with memories, none of them good ones. He had also had to spend them sober, having finished the bottle of rum on Tuesday evening after being unable to sleep. The letter had unsettled him and brought years of bitterness to the surface. He had nearly killed Thomas Deacon himself, but confirmation of his demise brought him no pleasure or satisfaction, despite everything that had happened.

But it was not the news of his death that had perturbed him, it was the fact that he had been invited to the reading of the will, with the assertion that it would be to his advantage to attend. He was still not completely sure whether he should go or not. Although should he decide to, how he was going to finish work in time to make Euston by 10.00 was another matter.

Having drunk himself to sleep on Tuesday, he had turned up for work on the following morning looking decidedly ill. Arthur had thankfully assumed he was just a bit under the weather, which was neither confirmed nor denied by Robert. Luckily Jim had kept quiet about their trip to the Bell the previous night; he was a good lad. Wednesday had been a horrendous day, but thankfully Jim had given him half of his lunch, which was fortuitous as otherwise he would have needed to wait until he got home to eat. Jim's Mum always ensured that he had plenty of lunch with him so it was no great hardship to him, and had gone some way in paying Robert back for all the beer he had bought the night before. The sandwich was everything he needed to quiet his upset stomach; lashings of butter and thickly cut cheese. It was the first thing that he had eaten for twenty four hours and had at least helped put a bit of colour back into his cheeks. After deliberating on Wednesday evening and all of Thursday, Robert had all but decided that he should go, having nothing to lose. The ticket was paid for, at least the ticket to Scotland was; he had assumed the details of the return journey would be clarified once he had arrived. The only issue remained making the short trip from his lodgings in Greenwich to Euston, which in itself would not normally be problematic. He would have to excuse himself from work, of course, and he would use the perceived illness he had had all week as an excuse for his absence. His empty wallet, however, meant that he would have to at least turn up initially in order to pick up his weekly wages, before suffering a sudden deterioration in his condition which would require immediate bed rest.

Upon entering the main building of Simpsons, Robert ascended the stairs and along the short walkway towards his office, stopping outside the door briefly to compose himself. He took a deep breath, hunched himself up into what can only be described as a walking foetal position and shuffled into the room, gingerly. "Bloody hell!" spluttered Arthur in shock, "what happened to you? Did you piss the bed?" It was eight thirty five, exactly twenty five minutes before Robert would normally have arrived for work. Arthur was, of course, sat at his desk already, working on the latest financial report that had been requested by his superiors, with Jim already hunched over his own desk feverously pawing through invoices.

"I haven't slept a wink, Arthur. I feel terrible. Whatever it is I've picked up I just can't shift it" he croaked. Sniffing and furrowing his brow, he leant against the doorframe and sighed forlornly, in a performance that the great Charles Laughton would have been proud of. Arthur peered over his reading glasses and viewed Robert suspiciously. Or so Robert thought, but that was merely paranoia fuelled by the fact that there was not a thing wrong with him other than severe hunger.

"Well *whatever* it is that you have got, I certainly don't want it! And neither does young James over there."

"Do what?" enquired James, distracted from his work by the mention of his name.

"I said you don't want it either do you?" Arthur repeated.

"Don't I? What's that then? What don't I want?" James enquired, confused by the sudden back and forth which had interrupted his concentration.

"Oh never mind, never mind", Arthur snapped, irritated by the whole episode. "Just get on with those bloody invoices!" Jim blushed and got his head down again over his work, the back of his neck turning a bright shade of crimson. Robert felt guilty, knowing how Jim hated it when Arthur got irritable, but staying in character, he made his way slowly to his desk and sat down.

"I'll just work through it Arthur, I'll be…I'll be…I'll be…." he stammered, imitating an imminent sneezing fit.

"You'll be what for heaven's sake?" Arthur snapped, now becoming most irked at the fuss being caused, as Robert unleashed a loud booming noise from the back of his throat and proceeded to knock a pile of papers off his desk in an attempt to disguise the fact that he had no more sneezed than he had lacked any sleep the previous night.

"For the love of God, man! Try not to infect the rest of us with your germs!" Arthur snapped. "Whatever's the matter with you today? Not only have you come in early and disturbed my routine, but you've now turned the office into a music hall farce. This is a place of work, of business, of peace and calm. It is not, I repeat not the bloody Aldwych and last time I checked you were not Ben bloody Travers. Now would you kindly settle down and give us all a bit of peace and bloody quiet so me and James can…." Robert looked at Arthur confused, wondering why he had stopped his rant, but the answer was not long in coming. Arthur rose to his feet, took his spectacles from the end of his bulbous, red nose, folded them and placed them in the pocket of his jacket. He paced over to James's desk, Robert's eyes following him from left to right, until he stopped and stood staring at James who had an invoice in his left hand and a sandwich in his right. "And what, pray tell, is that, young James?"

James stopped chewing, swallowed and slowly turned his head towards Arthur's. "Cheese and piccalilli", he replied.

"I don't give a blooming hoot what's in it. It could be bloody venison for all I care. What I mean, young James, is what the bloody hell are you doing sat there eating it for?"

Jim, despite having already cleared his mouth, swallowed hard, grimaced slightly and said "because I'm peckish."

Arthur, leant down till his nose was an inch away from Jim's. "It's," Arthur glanced up at the clock then back into Jim's eyes, "eight forty four. Lunch is at one o'clock sharp. Not a minute before and not a minute after! Now be a good lad and…" Arthur stopped again and swallowed, "what did you say was in that?"

Jim smiled, proudly, "Cheese and piccalilli, Arthur" he replied.

"Mr Treadwell, to you" said Arthur, eyeing the contents of Jim's right hand.

"Sorry Arth…I mean, Mr Treadwell. It's cheese and piccalilli. My mum makes it herself." Jim was now positively bursting with pride at the interest Arthur was showing in his lunch.

"Of course she makes it for you. I didn't think you'd be making sandwiches yourself, not with bread cut that finely. That's a mother's hand that's cut that," said Arthur, who had now stood up and had begun rocking back and forth on his heels, with both thumbs in his jacket pockets and his fingers tapping on the sides of his stomach. "Oh yes, Mrs Treadwell makes a lovely sandwich, so she does. Friday today, that'll be tongue and mustard. My favourite."

"No," said James, "I mean she makes the piccalilli herself." Arthur cocked his head and his eyes widened with interest.

"Does she really, young James? Well she sounds like a fine woman and that piccalilli does smell tasty; very tasty indeed," said Arthur, swallowing again.

Robert hadn't eaten a proper meal in days and hadn't yet had breakfast that morning. He wished that they would stop keep talking about food as it was doing nothing to help his empty stomach, yet the conversation continued unabated. "It's all about the balance between the mustard and vinegar, my mum says. It makes it nice and punchy. You sure you don't want to try some, Mr Treadwell?"

Arthur shook his head and protested. "No, no. Don't be silly, lad. You enjoy it" he said, swallowing again and staring intently at it. "You enjoy it; but not until lunchtime, mind. There's a good lad, put it away and get on with those invoices while I get on with my tongue and mustard, I mean my report." Robert's plan was not turning out as expected, but as he sat there leant against his fist, wondering what his next move was, the constant food references got the better of him and his stomach groaned, aching at the thought of one of Jim's sandwiches. Upon hearing the loud noise, Arthur turned to look and Robert seized on his opportunity, putting one hand on his stomach and the other up to cover his mouth. "Ooh God I think I'm going to be sick," Robert spluttered, making fake retching noises. Jim quickly packed his sandwich up in his thick brown paper parcel, whilst Arthur pursed his lips together tightly and held his breath whilst retreating to behind his desk.

"You best get home, Robert," said Arthur whose face was grimacing at the thought of catching whatever foul illness he thought Robert had succumbed to.

"Are you're sure, Mr Treadwell? Can the work wait till next week?" asked Robert, with as much concern as he could muster.

"Never mind the blooming work, just get out, and here…" Arthur pulled an envelope from his desk and gave it to Robert, "there's your wages, now off home to bed and don't come back till you've got rid of it."

Robert shuffled out of the room, one hand clutching his stomach, the other grasping at his pay packet. He had to move quickly; firstly back to his rooms to pick up his suitcase, having had no choice but to leave it there whilst going to work with the appearance of intending to stay there for the day. Once at a safe distance from the view of his office window, Robert hastened his journey back home until he was running full pelt. Once there he dropped his jacket and ran to have a quick drink of water after the run home had left him parched. He grabbed the luggage that he had left conveniently by the door and put on his jacket, then tapped the pocket to check he had got the letter in case he had any difficulties upon his arrival in Scotland. He had already checked it several times that morning, but what lay ahead made him nervous and he was conscious that once he was on the train it would be too late to turn back. He shut the front door and made his way down the street towards the station, tapped his pocket once more, then stopped, rolled his eyes and cursed himself. He tore back up the street, through his front door and picked up the envelope containing his wages that had fallen from his pocket when he dropped it. His nervous habits irritated him but sometimes he was pleased about them, the constant checking of things had prompted him to remember something was amiss, and without the envelope he would spend another day hungry. And after all the talk of sandwiches already this morning, his stomach would have to be his first priority once he had successfully arrived at Euston.

Owing to the delays in the office, Robert found himself desperately short of time and upon arriving at Greenwich train station realised that the next train would not have arrived at Euston until five past the hour. As such his wage packet was immediately being eaten into as he found it necessary to hail a hackney carriage in order to get to Euston for ten o'clock. The drive was only eight miles long and, thanks to the Blackwall tunnel, was a lot quicker than it had been previously. However, due to the rise in commercial vehicles utilising the link between the two sides of the river, Robert still found himself sweating as the time rapidly approached the hour. His hunger had abated and given away to the stress of missing the train, although his stomach still continued to growl. The driver looked over his shoulder into the back of the car, throwing Robert a quizzical look. "Crikey, is that your stomach? I thought it was my engine at first." It permeated through Robert's trance-like state and interrupted thoughts of what was in store for him; a long train journey, albeit one with a dining car thankfully, of a weekend of Scottish hospitality and of an answer to the question of his inclusion.

"Yes, sorry", replied Robert, "I haven't had time to eat yet. Speaking of time, I'm a bit pushed for it. I'm catching a train at ten and it's the only one till tomorrow so any chance you might get the speed up a bit?"

The driver looked visibly hurt at what seemed to Robert to be a perfectly reasonable request. "I'm going as fast as I can, guv. Honest. I know the old thing's not as good as these new low loaders that Austin have just bought out, but it's as good as you're gonna get this side of the water. You wanna think yourself lucky you didn't get Old Sid pick you up; he's still driving an electric cab.

It's the only hummingbird I know still running but the stubborn bugger won't part with it." Robert wished he had not mentioned anything. "We're nearly there anyway, guv; two more minutes." A glance at his wrist watch told Robert that this would give him an additional five minutes to make his way to the correct platform and find his train.

The promised two minute journey turned out to be four, so having paid the precise amount to the driver, much to his displeasure; Robert sprinted through the crowded station towards platform four. His legs, having only been used for sedate strolling for many years, started to burn as the lactic acid soared through his muscles and his chest felt like it would explode at any moment. He weaved through the passing hustle and bustle; men in suits, couples day tripping in the capital, a group of school children in smart blue uniforms and straw boaters being led by a very nervous looking bespectacled woman. Dodging a yapping dog intent on nipping his ankle as he ran past it, and vaulting a pile of luggage being pushed by a porter on a barrow, he could now see the heavy doors of his train being slammed shut for the final time; the conductor readying his flag to signal to the driver that it was safe to leave. "Ticket please, sir", bellowed a uniformed man at the turnstile, but Robert did not even acknowledge him, choosing to bustle past him instead at pace. He neared the end of the train just as it began to pull away, after the conductor had blown his whistle and waved his flag. "Hey, you there! Stop and show your ticket", came a cry behind him, but Robert was not going to miss the train. Sprinting up the platform and pulling up alongside the end carriage, he grabbed at the handle of the door and twisted until it flew open, whilst gritting his teeth as the pain gripped his hamstrings and his lungs burned. He threw his luggage onto the floor of the carriage and with as much energy as he could muster, leapt torso first aboard the train which had just started to pick up more speed. There was a mixture of confusion and amusement from the onlookers on platform four, as the train left the station with two legs dangling from the last carriage and its door swinging freely. On board the train, Robert was helped to his feet by a steward who then managed to lean out of the train and shut the door.

Leant over with one hand on his knee and the other against a seat to steady himself, Robert panted, unable to control his breathing after the most effort he had exerted in as long as he could remember. "Are you ok, sir?" The steward enquired. "You really ought not to have done that, sir. It's ever so dangerous." Robert continued to pant, unable to speak just yet. "I'm afraid I'm going to have to ask you for your ticket too, sir. This train is for ticket holders only. If you haven't got a ticket I'll have to inform the conductor."

Robert took a deep breath, steadied himself and stood up. "It's fine" he said, reassuring the steward. "I've got a ticket. Hang on a second will you." Robert patted his jacket, feeling the reassuring presence of both his wallet and his paperwork. He reached inside and pulled out his ticket, satisfying the steward that he was merely tardy as opposed to being a stowaway.

"Thank you, sir" replied the steward, "I'll show you to your seat once you've caught your breath."

As he took the ticket back from the steward and put it back safely in his pocket, he surveyed his surroundings for the first time. The carriage seemed small, although that could just have been due to the shame he felt as three pairs of eyes stared back at him with a mixture of embarrassment, amusement and disgust. A slim woman, slight of build looked at Robert with blushed red cheeks, whilst the older woman next to her muttered something under her breath and looked at him with scorn. The older woman wore an expensive green dress and was bejewelled from head to toe, the most extravagant adornment being a huge diamond ring on her wedding finger. Robert looked back at the younger woman and smiled at her, causing her to blush further and shift in her seat. "I'm sorry if I've caused you any disruption, ladies", he said, smiling sweetly at the older woman to try and placate her.

"Perhaps you can leave us alone now then?" she said, looking down her nose at Robert. The younger woman looked even more uncomfortable at this comment.

"Of course, I'll leave you be." Robert said, realising his presence was not welcome any further. But before he could say any more, a voice behind him left him in no doubt as to his next move.

"Well get a bloody move on then! This compartment is full and you're bothering these good ladies. Bloody cheek if you ask me." Robert turned and saw a man of similar age to him, dressed in an expensive suit which belied the rest of his appearance and behaviour. His hair was greased into a parting and he sported a thin moustache but was otherwise clean shaven. He seemed very much like he was merely portraying the act of a gentleman, which despite his tailored suit and impeccably shined shoes, his manners and East London accent betrayed him quite transparently.

Robert had the measure of him in an instant, but wished not to cause any more of a disturbance, so proffered his apologies once again and departed the carriage. Glancing back as he shut the door, he saw the man leaning into the bejewelled woman, touching her knee and fawning over her as if she had been damaged by Robert's entrance. The young woman looked uncomfortable and looked to the floor, whilst the fourth passenger, who Robert had failed to notice at the time, continued to read his broadsheet, with only a scruffy pair of brown brogues and the bottom half of a caramel coloured suit on show. The man had not let Robert disturb him from being enveloped in paper; the front page reporting on a devastating underground explosion at Lidgett Colliery in Barnsley, as well as tensions growing over the expected Italian invasion of Abyssinia. The porter led Robert along the train, which rattled and then lurched, unbalancing Robert and forcing him to grab hold of the handrail for support. According to the paper, across the Atlantic, Howard Hughes was in the process of attempting to break the air speed record, hitting over three hundred and fifty miles an hour; whilst the train was sluggish in comparison, travelling at just over one hundred miles an hour. The porter had no such trouble walking unaided, clearly well practised in the art of staying on his feet. "Stop!" Robert said suddenly. The Porter turned round to see him nod towards the dining cart, "here will do!"

Despite the fact that the shenanigans in terms of getting onto the train had made his body ache, and left him feeling sick, the over whelming sense of hunger was still the pervading feeling within him. The porter led him through the dining cart and showed him to an empty table. Upon sitting, he had a bright white linen serviette extravagantly unfurled over his lap by a waiter who had appeared out of nowhere and was immediately offered a menu. Whilst the waiter offered advice on what he would recommend food-wise, the porter lingered, but for what purpose Robert was not too sure of. "Oh, thank you!" said Robert to the porter, who smiled, sardonically, and departed tip-less. Robert glanced at the smoked salmon and scrambled egg, served with wholemeal toast and butter that the waiter was coercing him to order and baulked at the price.

The waiter, noting Robert's lack of awareness with the Porter as well as the look of horror at the price of the food, began to modify his expectations. "If smoked salmon isn't to sir's liking, we do an excellent cup of coffee."

Whilst Robert was not about to waste what most people earn in a day just on a breakfast, equally he needed to eat and objected to being made to feel degraded. Quite why people felt the need to make others feel unworthy was beyond him and Robert had always hated snobbery. It was a horrible enough trait in the privileged, which he had been sick of in his school years, but it seemed even worse coming from the unprivileged. As the waiter stood with an expression suggesting he had a bad smell under his nose, Robert found a balance between not being profligate and over full, but filling himself and putting the waiter in his place. "I'll have poached eggs with sausage, toast and butter and a coffee please."

The waiter smiled through gritted teeth, "very good choice, sir. Leave it with me", he replied, bowing slightly and then scurrying up the walkway towards what Robert assumed was the cooking area. Quite how the chef managed to produce such an array of different foods, in such a tiny area with the train travelling at such speed was beyond him, but he was keen to sample his efforts as soon as possible.

Within a minute, the waiter had appeared again carrying a pot of coffee and poured a cupful, without spilling a drop, again amazing Robert at how expertly the staff coped in the conditions. Declining milk and sugar, much to the dismay of the waiter, he sipped on the coffee, the strength of which hit the back of his throat and immediately made him feel better. Strong black coffee in the morning was as pleasurable to him as strong alcohol was to him in the evening, enjoying the bitterness and richness that the lack of milk and sugar provided. He was now definitely ready for food, with his body rested, except for some painful ribs from his grand entrance, and his stomach settled. He could have done with a newspaper to read, but instead settled into glancing around the dining cart and amusing himself at some of the sights.

In the main, the carriage was full of suited men, dining alone, such as him, but Robert imagined a back story for each one he could see. The man to his right was married; he had kissed his gargantuan wife goodbye on the cheek this morning and grimaced at her breath which smelt of kippers and runny, undercooked eggs. She wore a vile flowered dress which was more like the vast tent one would find at a circus and he despised her. He was on his way to Carlisle, the only stop between London and Scotland, where he would meet his mistress and engage in 3 days of unbridled passion at a seedy bed and breakfast. Booked in under Mr and Mrs Smith, he and his young companion would dream of being together and hatched a way of making it possible. They had decided on murdering his wife, inheriting her fortune, which had been his only reason of marriage in the first place, and setting up a new life together. After the three days they parted, again, and he returned to his hideous life and rekindled his tedious marriage with no intention or guts to carry through his dastardly plan. His mistress would continue to wait for him patiently, hanging on to his promises.

The man sat one table up the dining cart away from Mr Infidelity, was only partially visible, but Robert saw enough to picture him perfectly. He was scrawny, wore thin rimmed spectacles and a pristine suit and his name was Charles. He was married but only in name, not in fact. He preferred the company of men and was on his way to Scotland for a clandestine meeting with a man named Archie, who he had been corresponding with for several weeks. Archie was handsome, thick set, rugged, enjoyed outdoors pursuits and sodomy. Upon arriving in Glasgow, Charles would know who Archie was as he would be wearing a carnation in his button-hole and standing under the station clock. Archie would know who Charles was as he would be holding a copy of The Times against his chest and have an umbrella open regardless of whether it was raining or not. The Police would arrest Charles upon his arrival as Archie was actually Police Sergeant McKay who posed as a homosexual in fake advertisements to lure out sodomites in a joint operation between London and Scottish Police. Charles would be sentenced to a term at His Majesty's pleasure, while Archie would continue to arrange further clandestine meetings with unsuspecting men.

One table further up, the man, no, the woman with her back to Robert, now then, who was she and what was her story? She had short bobbed hair, in perfect blonde curls. Robert could see the back of her neck. He could not see her face at all, but she was beautiful, with sparkling eyes as deep and blue as the ocean. Her complexion was fresh and unblemished, and her nose elegant and slender. She had a beautiful smile which lit up her face but which hid an underlying sadness, but Robert could not quite decide what it had been caused by. He approached her; she turned and looked startled initially but then was pleased to see him stood in front of her. She smiled seductively and he leant in and kissed her passionately on the lips. His heart filled with warmth and blood surged into his penis which suddenly gorged, reawakened after being redundant for so long. He gazed into her eyes; she was as beautiful as he imagined, with a perfect face and long, gracefully thin neck. The dress she was wearing seemed hardly appropriate, showing her décolletage fully, with her buxom, heaving bosom bringing out an animal urge in Robert that he had not felt in as long as he could remember. He wanted her, physically, mentally and spiritually; she was perfect. She stared intently into his eyes, appearing to feel the same longing and yearning as he did. She smiled, parted her sultry lips to show her perfect teeth and said "Scrambled egg and sausage, sir. Would you care for more coffee?" Robert, stunned back into reality, looked up at the waiter who looked impatient at his lack of response. "Would you like more coffee, sir?" he said, haughtily.

"Oh, yes, sorry, yes I would, thank you." The waiter placed the plate in front of Robert, who picked up his cutlery and immediately began inhaling egg and sausage with gusto. Remembering himself, he put his cutlery down, swallowed and thanked the waiter, who had refilled his cup with coffee and was already walking away towards the empty table that previously had Robert's impeccable blonde sat at it. The table was now empty, with only cutlery and crockery and a plate with money on it as a reminder of who had occupied it. The waiter picked up the plate of money, quickly examined it, rolled his eyes then began clearing the rest of the table. Robert had already decided he would not be tipping the waiter. He had spent enough on breakfast already, and once he had left the dining cart he did not much care for what the waiter thought of him, after all he would not see him again.

His breakfast had been eaten in full with barely a crumb left to remind him of it. He had enjoyed but had barely tasted it; such was the speed in which he consumed it. He took the last swig of coffee to wash his breakfast down with, left the precise amount to settle the bill on the table and made to leave before the waiter came back. At least he would not have to face him while he realised he had not been tipped. On that matter, Robert resolved to find his own seat, rather than finding a porter to do it for him, to avoid a repeat of the previous awkwardness. Glancing at his ticket it seemed fairly straight forward, the seat and carriage being clearly marked. He made his way through the dining cart towards the front of the train, just in time to enter the adjoining carriage as the waiter appeared with a plate of food, although not swiftly enough to avoid a glare from the bejewel woman who had been so offended by him earlier. She had been sat alone and sneered at Robert as he passed, stopping only to thank the waiter for placing a plate of ham and eggs in front of her. "Lucky bitch!" Robert thought to himself; despite his own meal he could have easily polished off another plateful.

Moving through the train he entered the carriage where he would find his seat, but right outside that compartment his movement was blocked by a man with his back to him. He recognised him immediately by the suit and the slicked hair as being the Cockney rogue with the gentleman's plumage. As he sidled past him he saw with surprise that he was pressed up against the timid young lady from the carriage, and was engaging in heavy petting with her. He had not imagined the two of them together at all, believing that all three were separate passengers, or if any were connected then surely it would have been he and the older lady, after all the fawning he had subjected her to. He felt a little aggrieved at this discovery, the man being so unpalatable, and her being such a pretty little thing. She was a little plain, of course, but Robert could see beyond that. She was naturally pretty, without the need of such extravagant jewellery that the older woman had been displaying; timid, in need of protection and of a strong, loving man. How on earth had she got wrapped up with that unpleasant fellow?

He wondered. But that was none of his business, and he passed by them into the compartment to finally take his seat.

Chapter Four

"How do I know for sure though?" she asked, cautiously. She was twenty four but had never been with a man, having followed her Mother and her Grandmother into service at the age of fourteen. As such, she was naïve to the machinations of the average male, let alone one so evidently well versed in the manipulation of a tender young girl. He leant against the side of the train, smirked and ran his fingers through his slicked back hair.

"You can trust me darlin', I'll look after yer. Yer don't want to be bowing and scraping to that snooty bitch for the rest of yer life, do yer?" She bit her lip and her eyes began to well up. "What's wrong darlin'? Hey, don't cry. You can trust me. Now you'd better get back to her, she'll be wondering where you are."

She wiped at her eyes, and straightened her dress out which had become wrinkled after he had finished pawing all over her. "It's fine. She's just ordered food and she asked me to watch her luggage while she was gone." She went to move away but hesitated. "You won't let me down will you?" she asked, desperate to trust him but reluctant to commit herself so freely.

"Trust me, darlin'. You let me work my magic, and we'll be set for life. You and me. What's wrong? You trust me don't yer?"

She sighed, "I want to, but, but my Mum warned me about men like you. 'Men only want one thing,' she said, and then you'll leave me once you've got what you want."

He put his hands to his chest inwardly and feigned as if she had offended him, "what me? Never, darlin'. I'd never hurt yer."

She frowned, but his cockney accent and little boy lost look ensured her concern was allayed and she smiled at him sweetly. "Okay. I trust you. But we've only just met. How can I be sure?" she pleaded innocently.

"Darlin' girl," he said, lowering his voice to suggest sincerity. "We may have only just met, but I know true love when I see it. Now run along and babysit her majesty's luggage. I need to do a bit of business. I'll see you back in the compartment." As she hurried past him he patted her on the backside and she squealed in surprise and cocked her head back at him, her elated grin portraying the signs of a girl in love; encapsulated at the emotion she had never felt before, swooning at the attention of her admirer. He blew her a kiss and smiled, and as she went through the door to the next carriage, his smile turned into a smirk. His charm had done the trick once again. She would be putty in his hands from now on; just how he liked it.

****

Robert was sat comfortably, staring out of the unusually large, low set window as the train climbed to the summit and passed through Tring station. The subsequent descent marked a distinct change in landscape as the chalky Chiltern Hills were replaced by a distinctively wilder, weathered, wooded area. His breakfast had finally hit his stomach and he was content, so closed his eyes and tried to relax. He had never been capable of sleeping during the day, even if he tried in the comfort of his own bed, so there was no chance of napping; but he resolved to at least rest as best he could for the remainder of the journey. As the train travelled from Hertfordshire into Buckinghamshire, it was plunged into darkness for what seemed like an eternity as it passed through Linslade tunnel. On the other side the scenery was breath taking and was a marked contrast to the busy, urban sprawl of the capital that Robert was used to. There was a vast array of pine and heather-clad hills, where animals could be seen grazing, giving way to areas of red sandstone. Regardless of the outcome of his foray into Scotland, he had at the very least been treated to the visual beauty of counties that he had never ventured into previously.

After passing through Buckinghamshire, the train was already in Northamptonshire, although despite feeling as though he had travelled a fair distance, the journey was merely a little over an hour long with at least six and a half to go. At least his travelling companions seemed far more sedate than those in the original carriage where he had entered so unceremoniously. To his left sat an elderly lady who had declined the opportunity of sitting next to the window due to her suffering from travel sickness. She had told Robert all about it the moment he sat down, along with a verbose version of her life story which had culminated in the train journey to Scotland where she would be visiting her daughter and her family. He had placated her by listening intently, showing all the correct reactions dependent on what part of her life she was detailing; smiling and laughing at stories of childhood and fun, frowning and sighing at stories of death and loss, smiling once more at her joy of seeing her granddaughter for the first time in years. She was harmless and her voice was quite soothing, so Robert was happy in letting her speak at him; although he was happier that she was now asleep. Opposite the elderly lady was a very stiff looking man who sat bolt upright in his seat and seemed content enough in just reading his paper. He was dressed impeccably with a shirt so starched, with creases so straight and sharp it looked uncomfortable to wear. His tie was worn with a perfect Windsor knot and his shoes were so shiny that the light from the vast window often caught them and reflected back into the compartment. He carried with him the air of someone who did not want to engage in banal chit chat, which is probably why the elderly lady seemed so pleased that Robert had entertained her narrative. Similarly uninterested in being interrupted was the studious young lady who sat to the left of the gentleman, who was as aesthetically pleasing to Robert as the view out of the window was. She had a rounded face with eyes the colour of cocoa and hair to match, cut into a stylish short bob. She had a long fawn coloured skirt to mid-calf length, with a matching jacket which had shoulder pads and butterfly sleeves, accentuating her slim waist and narrow hips. She was engrossed in a book and had not even looked up at Robert when he entered and took his seat, and was seemingly completely oblivious to the conversation that ensued.

Continuing to look out of the window, interrupted only by Kilsby tunnel which once again plunged the train into darkness, Robert's journey now took him into Warwickshire where the scenery had become distinctly industrialised. It was at this point, ironically after miles and miles of beautiful countryside, that his pretty travelling companion chose to look up from her book and gaze out of the window. He took this opportunity to break the ice with her. "It reminds me of London; all smoke and smog." She smiled politely and buried her head back in her book, whilst undeterred, Robert tried again. "Any good?" he asked, nodding at the book.

She peered over it and raised an eyebrow, knowing that he could not care less whether it was good or not, but merely wanted to engage her in conversation. But she answered nevertheless, being polite and wanting to avoid any awkwardness for the remainder of the journey. "It's wonderful, yes. I saw it being performed at Notting Hill Gate in the summer and simply had to buy it so I could read it for myself."

Robert sensed that her love of the book would keep her talking, so continued on the subject. "What's it about?" She raised her eyebrow again at him. Robert looked at the book, "Murder in the Cathedral by T S Eliot," he read out loud. "Okay, so it's about a murder in a cathedral. But who gets murdered in a cathedral?"

She looked alarmed at him. "Who on earth do you think?" she asked.

"I've no idea; I'm not reading it, am I?" he replied, playfully.

She sighed and looked disappointed at his lack of knowledge. "Thomas Becket, of course! It focuses on the days leading up to his horrendous murder in Canterbury Cathedral but…"

"Hence the title", Robert interjected, at which she rolled her eyes.

"Naturally. But the really clever thing is although it's set well over seven hundred years ago, its message resonates in today's society. Essentially it's a tale of one person's struggles against authority; it just so happens that Eliot uses Becket as the vessel that carries that message." Her passion for the book made her animated, breaking down the exterior that had previously been impervious to him.

"I see," said Robert, not really understanding. "So the clever bit being….?"

"For heaven's sake, man!" she replied, exasperated. "Look at history. Women died for the right to vote not even twenty years ago. Look what can be achieved when one person decides that enough is enough. You start off with one lone voice and it can turn into a huge movement. Look what's happening in Italy now."

There was silence, Robert felt out of his depth, having paid little attention to politics which had little or no interest to him. Then remembering the front of today's paper, "Oh yes, Abyssinia. Sorry, no I don't understand, what's that got to do with anything?" he asked, knowing that the more he spoke the bigger the divide grew between them intellectually.

"The rise of Fascism, of course." She continued, passionately. "The Italians need stopping otherwise where will they stop invading? And if they can get away with it, what's stopping other countries from doing the same?" As she spoke, Robert noticed the gentleman next to her fidget in his seat, uncomfortably. It was the first sign of a reaction from him after he had displayed as much movement and emotion as a waxwork mannequin previously. "We should send our military over to help otherwise who knows where it will end. Another World War probably!"

Suddenly the gentleman sat next to her folded his paper under his arm, stood up and left the compartment. She glanced over as he shut the door, "was it something I said?" she wondered.

"I don't know," he replied. "He did look a bit uncomfortable. Perhaps he is related to Mussolini." At that she roared with laughter, rocked forwards and touched his leg, the realisation of which stopped them both in their tracks and their eyes fixed on each other. She smiled at him and pulled her finger off his leg towards her but lightly scraped her nail against him as she did so. It sent shivers down his leg and up into his stomach as she did it. Where had she learnt to do that? he wondered.

She leant back in her chair and resumed reading her book, just as a voice next to him said "I think I lost myself for a second there. Where was I? Oh yes, my granddaughter, Margaret. Pretty little thing, she is, ever so clever…" Robert, smiled at her ruefully. Whilst the young woman put her book in front of her face to avoid being dragged into the conversation, Robert could see her shoulders gently shaking as she silently giggled at his misfortune.

As Robert pandered to further stories of a family he had never met, his mind moved on to the man who moments ago felt it necessary to leave the compartment. Clearly he did not mind conversation per se as he had seemed oblivious to the elderly lady's stream of consciousness for some time before she had fallen asleep.

Perhaps he was jealous of the fact that he had been flirting with the young girl, or at least attempting to. They had not been speaking about anything contentious, unless he vehemently disagreed with her interpretation of the book she had been reading, but that was unlikely to provoke such a response. They had not really spoken about anything else, unless he was of Italian origin, but again that seemed unlikely given his complexion and general demeanour. As he had walked through the train, Robert had noticed that each compartment seemed fully occupied so it was unlikely that he had found another seat. On that basis he assumed that he would return at some point and prepared himself for it. He hated awkwardness or confrontation so he resolved to try and make the remainder of the journey as non-eventful as possible.

  Robert sat switching his attention between the elderly lady, staring freely at the young lady's breasts undetected, thanks to her eyes being hidden behind her book, and wondering where the stuffed shirt had disappeared to. The gentleman in question had made his way to the dining cart; it was midday, the time he took his lunch every day, punctually. He was shown to a freshly made table by the waiter who, despite working tirelessly through breakfast, had now seamlessly switched to the lunchtime service. "Good afternoon, sir. Here is the menu. May I draw sir's attention to the minute steak, flash fried in herb butter and served with straw potatoes, vegetables and a béarnaise sauce."

  The gentleman nodded, "Sounds first rate, I'll take it rare." The waiter looked on approvingly, after his suggestion had been accepted without the need to look at the rest of the menu.

  "And would sir care to take a look at the wine list?" The waiter purred, suspecting this particular customer would most definitely be leaving a handsome tip.

  "Why not, the sun must be over the yardarm by now!" He took the wine menu, and looked at it briefly, "I'll have a bottle of claret. That will go down nicely with the steak!" The waiter smiled and nodded his approval, then scurried off to the back of the carriage to dust off the wine.

  The gentleman gazed out of the window. He had enjoyed the attention paid to him by the over-zealous waiter, but now had the appearance of solemnity once more. The train had passed through the coal mines and quarries of Warwickshire, broken up only by lonely rural country homes and archaic churches partly hidden by trees. As the train entered into Staffordshire it was ten past twelve and in a little over two hours they had travelled one hundred and sixteen miles since leaving Euston. He looked lost in thought until the waiter bounded up to him, eager to please like a faithful puppy, carrying a bottle of wine which he had wrapped in a linen serviette collar to catch potential drips after being poured. "You can take that off, I'm not a child. Plus if I pay for a decent bottle of claret I want to be able to see the label to make sure it's not a bottle of cooking wine!"

The waiter, suitably admonished, removed the napkin. "Why of course, sir. I would never dream of such a thing." He poured a small drop to cover the base of the glass, at which the gentleman rolled it around and took a deep lungful, savouring the aroma, then drained the glass, swilling the wine in his mouth and swallowing, whilst the waiter looked on nervously.

"Fill her up" he ordered; the waiter smiled and nodded and duly poured, placing the bottle on the table and assuring the gentleman that he would return shortly with his steak. "Good show, old chap" came the reply, as the waiter scurried back towards the kitchen area, whilst the gentleman resumed his solitude. At the adjacent table, the bejewelled lady looked on at the gentleman while she waited for her coffee.

"So nice to see a man of class" she said. "It makes a change to some of the riff raff that were in here earlier." He nodded and smiled at her, which was perceived to be sufficient an invitation to join him at his table, bringing an empty wine glass with her. The man looked surprised at how forward she had been, but his manners and breeding ensured that he accommodated her.

"I probably shouldn't drink the whole thing at this time of day. I'll end up falling asleep, although at least that will make the journey go a bit faster!" He picked up a spare glass, the tables all being laid for four as standard, and filled it generously. "I'll use a clean glass, save spoiling it by mixing the grapes", he said, eyeing an empty bottle of white wine upside down in an ice bucket on the table she had just left.

"That'll do, that'll do! Otherwise you'll have me talking about my old mother, and that will never do", she said winking at him.

The two passengers engaged each other in polite conversation, whilst the waiter appeared at the table next to them carrying a pot of coffee and looked confused at the empty table. "How dare she!" he said, disapprovingly. "She's left without paying the bill."

"Has *she* now?" came the female reply behind him. At that the waiter turned round and looked embarrassed. "You can forget the coffee. I waited that long I've moved on! Oh and you can fetch my bill for me, after removing the coffee from it, of course."

The waiter bowed and shuffled backwards, remaining hunched over, retreating up the aisle towards the kitchen. "And any sign of my steak?" added the gentleman.

"Right away, sir, right away" the now flustered waiter replied before retreating into the kitchen. The two of them laughed heartily, his being a deep snorting, whilst hers was a coarse, cackle that suddenly seemed out of place compared to her appearance. He spotted it immediately and winced. She had taken a mere two sips of wine, but on top of what she had already consumed, she seemed to be slurring slightly and her accent had slipped into quite an unrefined tone, with a whiff of south London about it.

She continued to sip her wine and attempt to beguile her companion; whilst he sat there wondering what he had gotten into. "My name's Florence, by the way. I'm off to Scotland with my maid, silly thing, you wouldn't like her at all, simpering little child. Otherwise I'm" she paused, "all alone in the world. What about you? Is there a Mrs…sorry I didn't catch your name…" at which he shifted in his chair uncomfortably.

"No, my wife," he paused, "I'm not married…anymore."

She pursed her lips and did her best to look sympathetic, "how terribly sad. When did she pass away?" Visibly uncomfortable, he looked out of the window, as if to search for an escape, and then back at her, realising there was no subtle way out of the questioning.

"Florence, you say? That's a unique name for someone so," he paused to select the most appropriate word, "so grand". She smiled, approving of his description, though to him, she was clearly not quite as she first seemed, and the more she drank the more he regretted inviting her over.

Back in his compartment, the gentleman's continued absence had not gone unnoticed and Robert continued to flit between his two female companions, one distinctly more captivating than the other. "She's a pretty thing isn't she?" The elderly lady said.

"I'm sure she is, if she's anything like her Grandmother," Robert replied, smiling.

"Flattery will get you everywhere," she laughed, "but I'm not talking about my Granddaughter."

Robert was lost, "But who are you referring to?"

The elderly lady smiled knowingly and tapped his hand. "I may be old and Lord knows I have no interest in men anymore. No, there was only one man for me and since my Ernest passed away, I have no interest in romance. Those days are long gone. But I'm no fool. I can see you looking over to her longingly." Robert felt warmth on the back of his neck. "There's no need to be embarrassed. It's a beautiful thing; young love." The young lady slowly pulled her book down from her face and eyed the old lady suspiciously; perhaps she had not been asleep for quite as long as they had thought. She looked as embarrassed as Robert felt, and her cheeks blushed slightly. She smiled coyly at the woman, which, Robert noticed, crinkled the end of her nose. Then she smiled at Robert and covered her face once again with the book.

"I always think that life seems so short", the old lady reflected. "I've been on this planet for nearly seventy years, and yet I still feel as if I were a young girl. So many things I haven't done, places to go, adventures to be had. Then I remember; I have no one to enjoy it all with any more. It seems such a waste. I enjoyed every day with my Ernest; I just wish I could have our time together again. And if I did I'd make sure that there was nothing left unsaid, nothing left undone, and no regrets. Because by the time you realise what you've missed it's already too late." All the while she spoke;

Robert and the young girl looked at each other whilst absorbing the old lady's rhetoric.

Her words hung in the air as the carriage briefly became silent. "I think I might go and have some lunch. Excuse me won't you," the young lady said, breaking the moment of reflection. And with that she closed her book and departed the compartment, closing the door behind her.

"Well", the old lady said to Robert, "don't just sit there. Go and join her, unless you want to hear more of my silly stories." Despite having already eaten only a short time before, Robert took his leave of her company and dashed down the train to catch up with the young girl.

"Hey! Wait" he called after her, prompting her to turn and face him. "You disappeared quickly. What's wrong?" Robert asked.

"Perhaps I didn't want to sit there whilst your friend discussed our *romance*" she said sarcastically.

"She was right though. You are pretty" Robert replied. Quite where this boldness within him had come from he was not sure. He was beyond the realms of what was normally comfortable behaviour; absconding from work; trains to Scotland off the back of a mysterious letter; flirting with a woman significantly younger than him. Flirting successfully as well it seemed.

"Oh am I now?" she said, grinning. "You're not so bad yourself. Well are you treating me to lunch or not? I'm starving!" She was so full of life and it had rubbed off on Robert, who was happy to follow her lead as he liked where it was taking him.

"Whatever you desire, madam" he said, feeling committed to his new found confidence. So wrapped up in the moment and head freshly filled with the old lady's sage words, he nearly leant in and kissed her. He even suspected that she would respond to him had he done so. But he dallied on the moment too long and missed his opportunity.

"Madam!" she laughed. "I've not been called that for a while!"

"Well what should I call you?" he asked.

"Betty will do. Madam is far too formal! Come on, I'm ravenous," she said, taking his hand and leading him down the train towards the dining cart.

****

Florence, having drunk two glasses of red wine, had now forgotten her cut-glass accent completely and was betraying her actual roots which were in fact in the heart of Deptford. Her now reluctant dining companion was focusing on trying to restrict her alcohol intake, which seemed to be aligned to the volume of her voice. The more she drank the louder she got, whilst the louder she got, the more uncomfortable he became. He was halfway through his meal, which had been spent fending of what he perceived to be prying questions, when he began to grow impatient. Her behaviour was an embarrassment to him and he had spent the last seventeen years trying to be as private as possible, quite why he had allowed her to invite herself to join him was beyond him and he cursed his unnatural act of hospitality. "That steak looks nice. Do you know what, I could go a bit of that myself. Let's have a bit." He winced at the very thought, and ignored her. "Come on. I won't bite" she said. "Unless you want me to?"

He dropped his cutlery and looked aghast at her, then in a low, discreet but clearly irritated voice said, "Good God woman, what has got into you? Kindly act with a touch more decorum, will you."

Undeterred she continued, "Come on, what's wrong with you? You must be lonely. You've forgotten what it's like to be with a woman. When did you say your wife died again?" His face, crimson with rage, twitched and veins protruded from his neck.

Robert appeared at the far end of the dining cart, led keenly by Betty. They approached the waiter to request a table before a loud booming voice barked, "She's not dead! Now will you kindly desist from your incessant questioning?" The whole dining cart fell into awkward silence as discreet passengers tried their best to ignore the outburst, whilst nosier ones looked on with keen interest. Robert and Betty stood yards away facing him, as his face contorted, his eyes burned with rage and his fists clenched tightly. Florence sat in shock, initially at his outburst, but as she looked at him, a slow realisation dawned on her and her mouth began to slowly open and her eyes widened in horror. His outburst, she realised, she had seen before. Many years ago, but she *had* seen it and she now remembered it clearly. She slowly raised her right arm towards him and extended her index finger into a pointing position.

"It's you" she whispered with trepidation, as his facial expression changed from anger to panic. "It's you" she uttered louder, still pointing. "It's you!" she cried. "I recognise you. How dare you show your face before me!" Now even the discreet passengers stared at what was unfolding before them. A hundred thoughts and emotions ran through his body; shock at being recognised after all these years; reliving his shame; embarrassment at dozens of eyes being trained upon him; and regret at having ever boarded the train in the first place.

He shot up from his seat before she could say any more and bolted past her down the aisle, knocking over the remainder of his bottle of claret in the process. Wine sprayed violently all over Florence, which made her jump and stained her dress. It then proceeded to gently flow from the neck of the bottle, covering the bright white table cloth in blood-red coloured wine, which seeped wider across the cloth towards her. She sat in shock, unsure what to do next; her dress was ruined and her skin was splattered with red beads which dripped slowly down her neck and chest and into her cleavage. Robert approached her, picking up the napkin that her erstwhile companion had discarded and offered it to her to wipe herself with. Whilst the waiter began clearing and stripping the table of a half-eaten meal, partly drunk wine glasses and claret-sodden linen, Florence gently dabbed at herself, trying to salvage what remained of her dignity.

Despite her previous behaviour towards him, Robert cast that aside and helped her to her feet. He gently led her through the dining cart towards her compartment, whilst Betty followed behind, wondering how he knew where to take her. Despite their intrigue, neither Robert nor Betty asked her any questions; they just did the decent thing and stayed with her until she was safely back to her seat. The man who had sparked such ire in her had gone in the opposite direction, but Robert insisted he saw her back all the way just in case. Upon entering the compartment, her maid stood up and began fussing over her, whilst her cockney companion stood up and glared at Robert. "You again! What now yer bloody clot. Look at the state of 'er."

Betty looked confused, whilst Robert tried to interject. Before he could explain though, Florence spoke in his defence, her faux upper class accent returning having been sobered slightly by her earlier shock. "It seems this young man has been misjudged. He was my knight in shining armour." She squeezed his arm, and looked warmly at him, which made Robert feel uncomfortable and the cockney irritated. His attempt to defend Florence being unwelcomed had irked him and he did not want Robert levering his way into proceedings. That was the last thing on Robert's mind though. "There appears to be a spare seat all of a sudden," Florence remarked. "There was someone sat there earlier reading the paper but he seems to have disappeared. Why don't you join us? I'm Florence, by the way." She held her hand out for Robert to kiss.

"That's very kind of you, Florence" Robert replied, choosing to lightly shake her hand, much to her disappointment. "But I have promised this young lady lunch, and I am a man of my word." The cockney breathed a sigh of relief, but Florence suddenly turned; she was not used to being spurned.

"What her? What's she got that I haven't? She wouldn't know what to do with you even if she tried." Betty looked disgusted, not only by the slur but by the sudden volte-face in her behaviour after they had come to her aid.

"If you'll excuse us," Betty said, calmly, "we'll be leaving. I hear they serve lovely wine in the dining cart." At that, Robert and Betty departed, whilst Florence burst into tears borne out of frustration and inebriation.

"For heaven's sake, girl, stop fussing over me. Go and fetch a wet towel so you can clean my dress" she barked. The young maid complied at once, in fear of further admonishment from her now manic mistress.

"Fetch a brandy for 'er as well will yer," he said, "and one for me while yer at it, darlin'." He sat her down and lavished her with the attention that she had been craving all afternoon, which calmed her down and soothed her ego. The wine had gone to her head and loosened her behaviour, which combined with the need for attention made her ripe for exploiting. "There, there darlin'. I'm 'ere. You don't need no clumsy oaf looking after yer. I've got everything yer need right 'ere."

She swooned under his pandering, relieved at the attention after experiencing rejection, which she was unaccustomed to. He stroked her cheek with his hand and leant in towards her, kissing her and stroking his hand down her cheek which made her shudder, continuing down her shoulder and arm and across her left hand, pausing on her ring finger, then lightly towards her fingertips. "Oh, my!" she uttered, "how delightful!" His moustache had made her wince slightly, being sharp against her upper lip. But she ignored it, and enjoyed the moment.

He smiled at her, "there's plenty more of that, darlin'. Don't worry about that. Come 'ere before she comes back with that brandy." As their lips touched again, their embrace was punctured by the sound of glass shattering. They both looked towards the carriage door to see Florence's maid stood looking on. A single tear slowly slipped down her left cheek. Her face was a picture of broken-hearted disillusionment, whilst her feet, anchored to the floor like lead weights, were covered in tiny shards of glass and wet with spirit. She had returned sooner than expected and had seen everything.

****

Robert and Betty were seated, perusing the menu, while normal service had efficiently been resumed in the dining cart. Linen had been replaced and fresh cutlery and glasses fastidiously laid, enabling them to be seated at the very table that had played host to the havoc just a few minutes previously. "What on earth was that all about?" Betty asked him.

"I have no idea," he replied, "probably best not to dwell on it." He continued to look at the menu. "Which wine do you want then?" he asked.

"I don't. But how did she know you? And why did that slimy man look so angry at you?" she asked, desperate to understand.

Robert blushed slightly and dodged the question. "But you said earlier that you wanted wine?"

Betty sighed in frustration. "That was just so that I could make her feel stupid after what she said about me. I don't even drink. Wouldn't know what to do with you indeed!" she said, clearly offended by Florence's insult.

Robert's interest piqued suddenly. "Oh, so what would you do then?" He liked the direction in which their conversation was going.

"Never you mind!" she replied, disappointing him. "Shall I have the pork chop or minute steak? Hmm. I can't make my mind up. What are you having, my knight in shining armour?" Betty said, mocking Florence's dramatic overtures towards him.

Robert smirked, noting a hint of jealousy from Betty, which pleased him! "I don't know. The lamb chops sound nice." He then winced as he looked at the price, but resolved to have what he wanted, reminding himself that parsimony was not the way to win a girl's heart.

"What was going on with her accent as well?" Betty enquired, reluctant to drop her inquisitive thought process. She spotted Robert frowning in confusion so explained herself. "Well, on the way to her seat, she sounded like she was born under the sound of Bow bells, but once she was with those other two, all of a sudden she sounded like the Queen! What's that all about?" she exclaimed, waving the menu around in animation as she spoke.

"Oh yes. You're right; I suppose she did now I think about it. I hadn't noticed at the time" Robert replied, trying to focus on the menu and move the conversation away from the rear carriage. "I think I'll have the lamb, I can't remember the last time I had it and you make me feel reckless. Lamb it is" he said, with a satisfied grin on his face.

"Lamb! How could you?" she replied, looking at Robert with a look of disapproval. "I never cook lamb unless I have to."

"Quite easily, it's gorgeous. Covered in mint sauce and gravy. Mmmm" he said licking his lips with anticipation. At that moment, the dining cart door opened and a tearful young girl ran past their table and through to the next carriage, closely followed by a man frantically chasing after her.

"That was those two" Betty said in a hushed tone. Robert looked confused again. "The two from the carriage with her majesty" she said impatiently at his lack of awareness at the drama that was unfolding before them.

"Her majesty?" Robert said confused.

"For heaven's sake! What's up with you? Your girlfriend! Mrs 'you wouldn't know what to do with her'. That was the two others from the carriage."

Robert sighed, "Look. I don't care. I made a fool of myself in front of them earlier. I was late for the train and had to jump into their carriage while the train was leaving. I ended up falling arse over elbow and made myself look an idiot."

Betty giggled, "Really?" she asked, her eyes alive with excitement, the sum of which made Robert's stomach light and fluttery.

"Yes really!" confirmed Robert, reluctantly. "So if it's all the same to you, I'd rather forget all about them. I don't much care for him, slimy-looking bloke that he is. And her majesty, as you call her, has shown that you can have as many jewels and as much money in the world but it doesn't buy you class." At that Betty nodded in approval and smiled at him, pleased that he had spoken ill of her. "The young girl seemed nice though. I liked her. But…"

Betty's satisfied expression changed suddenly to one of disapproval. "But what?" she enquired, keen to know more.

"But nothing." he reassured her. "Look. I'm here with you aren't I? In case you haven't noticed…"

Betty waited for more, "go on" she prompted.

"I like you. I like you a lot, in fact. I think you're pretty. I think you're fascinating. I haven't met anyone like you for such a long time. I'd like to get to know you more." He swallowed nervously, having committed himself completely.

She smiled at him. "Aren't you sweet?" They sat in silence for a while gazing into each other's eyes, lost in thought and completely comfortable in each other's company, blissfully unaware at what was going on around them and who was passing by them this way and that.

Having ordered lamb chops for himself, and a pork chop for Betty, with all the trimmings, naturally, the two continued to become better acquainted. The more he listened to her, the more he absorbed and he wanted to know everything about her. He was fascinated by her and wished he had met her years ago. Whenever the conversation switched to her asking about him, he immediately asked her another question about herself. He felt that despite being several years older than her, he had lived half the life that she had and he wanted to avoid telling her about the tedium of his working at Simpsons, drinking in The Bell and, well, not much else. He certainly did not want to talk about the war. Betty was content in sipping at cold water, whilst Robert had ordered a bottle of beer for himself, partly because he wanted one or two to accompany his lamb, but mostly due to requiring it for Dutch courage. Spurred by the words of his elderly companion still ringing in his ear, he resolved to win Betty's heart and felt better equipped to do so with something to settle his nerves. "Blimey, you're thirsty aren't you?" she said as he drained half of his second beer.

"You could say that! You sure you don't want anything stronger than water?" Robert said, feeling suddenly uncomfortable at drinking alone, and being concerned at what Betty might think.

"No thanks. I prefer to have a clear head. Who knows what I might do if I have a drink. Might be something that I regret, eh!" Robert sensed that she liked him, but her words hung in the air unanswered, and there was an element of awkwardness all of a sudden. No doubt he would think of something clever to say in reply later when it was too late, he thought to himself. Nerves started to get the better of him and he downed the rest of his drink while Betty looked on, quite taken aback at the rate in which he was drinking.

"Excuse me a minute, won't you" Robert said, getting up to leave.

"Something I said? I have a habit of that today, making men get up and leave!" Betty replied, smiling at him.

Robert laughed nervously, "Not at all. Nature calls, that's all. I'll be back in two minutes, don't worry!" and he excused himself and made his way to the front of the train to find the toilet, leaving Betty alone to wait for the food to be served.

****

Florence sat patiently waiting for her admirer to return. There was not much she could do about the state of her dress which was covered in red wine all over the front, but she had unfastened the top two buttons to reveal her cleavage in order to tease more affection from him. She fluffed at her hair to make it neater and sat facing away from the door and gazing out of the window. On his return she would spin round at him and he would be awe struck at how she looked, although quite why he ran after the silly girl was beyond her. Who cares that she saw them kissing anyway, she thought to herself. She would mind her own business or find another job. Fancy being so shocked anyway. Surely she must have had one of the servants at her by now.

The train clattered along and she looked at the view of the Cheshire salt fields, growing inpatient, when at last the door opened. She smiled seductively and uttered, "I thought you'd abandoned me." As she turned, her face changed, "How on earth?.........."

She did not finish her question but stared open-mouthed with a look of confusion on her face as the figure stood before her. Slowly, her eyes dropped from their face to their right hand in which was held a steak-knife from the dining cart. She shook her head, her face twisted in terror, unable to speak, her voice trapped in her throat as they slowly walked towards her.

Chapter Five

Robert opened the toilet door and to his immediate surprise came face to face with the young maid, who was splashing her face with water and panting uncontrollably. "Oh, I'm ever so sorry," he said apologetically, retreating back into the corridor. Then remembering the melee in the dining cart earlier when she was seemingly being chased by the odious slick-haired cockney, Robert felt obliged to ensure she was okay. He gently pushed the door open, and she stood facing him, with tears still streaming down her face in a state of bewilderment. "I'm sorry for the intrusion, but the door was unlocked" he said. "Is everything alright? I saw you earlier in the dining cart and you seemed distressed." She continued to sob and collapsed backwards onto the closed toilet seat in a crumpled heap. "Do you want me to leave you to it?" Robert asked, unsure what to do in situations that involved highly emotional women and trying desperately to forget his full bladder.

"NO! Please don't. I don't want him to find me," she pleaded. "I don't know what to do. I don't know what I've done. Oh God, what have I done?"

****

Betty sat sipping her water, staring up and down both lengths of the dining cart waiting for Robert to return, but there was no sign of him. The dining cart had started to empty as the lunch service began drawing to a close. There were now only a handful of people left after the sudden surge of activity during the early part of the afternoon. The sound of a door opening made Betty turn round, but instead of Robert's return, it was the waiter carrying two plates in his left hand and an oval silver dish containing potatoes and vegetables in his right. "Pork chop?" asked the waiter; still as jovial and keen as he had been at the start of the journey. Betty nodded indicating the dish was hers, which the waiter placed in front of her after having already positioned the silver dish in the middle of her and the place where Robert had been seated. "Shall I keep the lamb warm until sir has returned?" the waiter asked.

"No, just leave it thank you. He'll be back in a minute" said Betty, who was now confused as to what was taking him so long. As further guests started departing the carriage, the sound of the door opening once again prompted Betty to spin around and once again it was the waiter. This time he approached her table proffering a gravy boat and a silver tray adorned with a paper doily atop which sat three ramekins; one of apple sauce; one of mint sauce; and one of English mustard. Betty sighed and smiled forlornly at him as he set the gravy and condiments down in the middle of the table.

"Will madam need anything else?" the waiter enquired, hovering over her.

Betty sighed and looked at the empty seat opposite her and replied, "No. I think madam has all of the food that she needs, thank you."

****

Trapped in the toilet, Robert was now too far into the process of trying to pacify the maid to withdraw and leave her, but he was acutely conscious of how long he had been away. So far he had been unable to get anything tangible from her by way of explanation, she just kept repeating the same thing over and over again, "What have I done? What have I done?" He had given her his handkerchief, which she had used to wipe her face and she had at least settled slightly. Although the offer to go and get her a brandy had unexpectedly set her off again, but Robert was unsure why.

"Look, perhaps I ought to take you back to your carriage," offered Robert, although the very thought of it filled him with dread.

"NO!" She pleaded. "No, please, don't take me there. I'll just stay here. I don't want to see him; or her. I'll just stay here. I'll be fine."

Robert, aware that he needed to draw his involvement to a conclusion and return to Betty, tried to facilitate an exit. "Look. I'm not sure what has happened, and it's none of my business, but I really have to go. Okay?" She began sobbing once more, and Robert groaned inwardly, now completely unsure as to what to do for the best. "I'm sorry," he said, "I hope it all works out for you." He turned and put his hand on the door handle, but at the prospect of him leaving her she jumped off the seat and pulled him around to face her. She pulled his face towards her and kissed him, which was the only way at that moment she could think of keeping him there to protect her. Robert, shocked by the sudden turn of events stood still on the spot. What may have been, several hours ago, a moment of delight, was now something that made him uncomfortable. But before he could pull himself away from her advances, the toilet door opened. Robert turned to see Betty stood looking at him with the maid hanging off him, her head resting against his chest and her arms around him.

"It's not what it looks like, Betty," he pleaded, "honestly. I was making sure she was okay and she just jumped on me." Betty was walking at a pace away from him, as he frantically tried to salvage the situation.

"It's fine," Betty said as she entered the dining cart, trying her hardest to be as indiscreet as possible, "you think she's pretty. You said so earlier. Go back to her; she looked like she was enjoying whatever it was you two were doing in the toilet." The waiter struggled to hide his amusement and an elderly couple their disgust. "Really I'm fine, although I think I'd rather eat alone now if it's all the same to you." She sat down and started cutting into her pork chop, whilst Robert sat opposite her, still pleading his innocence. "This is nice" said Betty, "but I was serious about what I said. Please take your lamb elsewhere. I have no interest in interrupting your little rendez-vous with that dainty little flower."

He was crestfallen and no amount of explanation was seemingly going to placate Betty. "Right!" he said. "Let's get to the bottom of this. Come with me." He stood and waited for her to follow him but Betty remained unmoved, chewing at her pork.

"Mmmm. There's sage in that gravy," she said, pretending to be unaffected. "And white wine. It's really rather good. Although I'm not sure how it would go with your lamb." Robert stared at her, intent on proving his innocence. "Fine" she said at last. "Say what you've got to say, or do what you've got to do and then leave me alone. Okay?"

Robert led her through the dining cart towards the rear of the train, intent on tackling Florence and the cockney and finding out what had led the maid to fear him leaving her. "You don't have to do this, Robert. I was just surprised that's all."

He stopped suddenly and faced her. "Betty, I've never met anyone like you. Please, you've got to believe me." He gripped her on each arm with his hands which were shaking at the emotion of the situation he was in. "I'll get the truth out of one of them and then you'll see. And we can start afresh and go back to our lunches and carry on with where we were headed."

Betty looked startled at his outpouring, and pitied him. "Oh, Robert, is that what you thought? Life's just not that simple, I'm afraid. It was fun; briefly, very briefly in fact, but what did you think was going to happen? We were going to have some lunch and that was it. You're a nice man, well at least I thought you were, but really, I'm not going to demean myself, fighting over you with that little girl." He looked deflated, but he remembered her blushing, her being irked with jealousy, and her finger running up his leg. He remembered the old lady's words of wisdom and resolved to fight for her, regardless of her protestations.

He pulled her by the hand, insisting on her following him into the rear carriage, and he refused to take no for an answer. They arrived at the rear carriage and immediately noticed broken glass and what smelt like Brandy all over the floor. He opened the end compartment door to see it empty, with the exception of Florence, who was laid against the side of her seat, facing the window with her eyes shut. "Great" he muttered, sarcastically. "I was hoping he'd be here." Betty stood, unimpressed at the door, wondering what Robert was intending to do now that the only occupant of the carriage appeared to be sleeping off her earlier excesses.

Before either one could say anything further, the conductor entered the compartment. "Anyone for Glasgow?" he queried.

Robert looked confused, "we all are, aren't we?" he answered.

"Rear coaches split at Lanarkshire from the rest of the train, Sir." The conductor explained, "The front coaches are for Glasgow.

Where's she for?" The conductor enquired, nodding towards Florence.

"I don't know," said Robert, "probably best to wake her and check though." He approached her to gently wake her up. He did not really care whether she was in the wrong carriage or not, but thought she might be able to shed some light on the maid's emotional state.

"There's no hurry, sir" the conductor said. "We're only just approaching Carlisle, but the crew change over here so I was just having one final check through. Are you alright, Sir?" He had noticed that Robert was stood, leant forward, examining Florence suspiciously.

"What's wrong, Robert" asked Betty, noticing the same as the conductor.

Robert's eyes had been drawn to her dress, which seemed in more of a mess than it had been previously. It was then that he had noticed the gaping wound in her chest and the fact that her cleavage was not merely splattered with red wine, but was covered in a violent mixture of claret and blood. He looked at Betty, flanking the conductor in the door-way; his face ashen white, and in a low, solemn voice, whispered, "She's dead."

Chapter Six

The conductor had asked Betty to go and fetch another member of staff to alert the Police, whilst he stayed in the carriage with Robert, ensuring no one else entered it. "May I ask what you and the young lady were doing in here before I arrived, Sir?" Robert, despite not wanting to divert attention on anyone in particular, found himself with no choice but to explain what he and Betty had witnessed previously and recounted it to the conductor. "I'll ensure the other members of the compartment are found, sir. Don't you fret about that."

Robert was not fretting, as such; he was more concerned with what the maid had been repeating over and over again. "What have I done? What have I done?" She did not look like she had it in her, he thought; to commit such a brutal crime. Far more obvious a suspect was the odious man who had been canoodling with her earlier and yet at the same time seemed quite put out when the victim had showed an interest in Robert. And what of the man from his own carriage, Robert thought. What had that altercation been about? The victim had said something about remembering him and that had provoked him to leave sharply enough to empty a bottle of wine all over the place. He looked like he had a bit of a temper about him as well.

At that moment, footsteps appeared outside the compartment, and upon looking, Robert saw the familiar face of the waiter approaching. "Your dinner is getting cold, sir. I've left the bill on the table too, if you wouldn't mind returning to your table." He was clearly worried that yet another guest had absconded without paying, after the previous altercation had left a minute steak and a bottle of claret as well as Florence's ham and eggs and a bottle of Chablis without fiscal resolution.

"Never mind that," barked the conductor, clearly irritated at the waiter's priorities in the face of the bloody mess that lay in the corner. "Now that you're here you can send for the Police." The train was just pulling into Carlisle, so time was of the essence; the train station providing the perfect opportunity to contact the authorities.

"That's why I'm here," the waiter responded. "This gentleman's," he paused and coughed into his hand, "lady friend alerted me to an issue here but did not actually specify what was required."

The conductor slapped the palm of his hand against his forehead, and then pointed at Florence's body in the corner of the compartment. "What do you bloody think the matter is?"

The waiter looked over at Florence's body and curled his lip up, "Yes well, I'm not surprised she's asleep after what she knocked back earlier. A right performance she made. AND her bill is still not paid."

The conductor, now almost apoplectic with rage, replied, "Well it's not likely to be either is it. She's been murdered you fool! Stabbed in the chest in broad daylight, it seems."

The waiter, unsure of where to look, such was his embarrassment, stared at the floor. "Here, these are my brandy glasses. What's happened to them?" he enquired, shuffling bits of broken glass around beneath his feet.

"I don't know." Robert replied, "They were here when we arrived. Someone must have dropped them I guess." The train began braking as it neared Carlisle station, causing Robert to hold on to the door for balance; the conductor and waiter needed no such assistance, however.

"That'll be that young girl" the waiter sneered, still irritated by his smashed glasses. "She's the only person to have had any brandy from me." The conductor was growing more and more frustrated at the waiter, who appeared oblivious to the fact that there was a murder victim yards from him.

"Enough about your brandy, Claude!" the conductor snapped. "Hop off here and inform the station master of what's occurred. Discretely mind. I don't want to upset any of the passengers. Perhaps if this young gentleman can stay and guard the compartment, I'll nip up to the driver and ask him to delay departure."

Left guarding the body of Florence, Robert sat trying to make sense of what was unravelling around him. If the maid was the only person to have bought brandy, then it made sense that she was the one who dropped the glasses outside the compartment. But what made her drop them? he wondered. What had she seen that was so shocking? Perhaps that was the cause of her fleeing through the dining cart. The loathsome man was following after her. Perhaps she had witnessed him murdering her? But then why would she have been saying "what have I done?" over and over again. Why would she not have just told Robert what she had witnessed? He would have to go and find her and get to the truth, but that would have to wait until either the conductor or the waiter returned to relieve him of his custodial duties.

  A man approached from the platform to enter the carriage, forcing Robert to block the door and apologise, telling him that a passenger had fallen ill and that he was expecting a doctor who would need privacy to examine her. Not a million miles away from the truth, as a doctor would be required to confirm death; although the open wound in her chest was a bit of a give-away. Robert decided it would be best to stand in the train door-way itself, to intercept any other passengers immediately. He stood looking up the platform waiting for the conductor to return, when he noticed a woman in a fawn dress walking towards the station exit. "BETTY!" He cried, desperate to attract her attention. Betty turned sharply at the sound of her name and saw Robert at the rear of the train, hanging out of the door. She turned and picked up her pace, ignoring him and continuing on her way towards the turnstile. Despite instructions from the conductor, Robert abandoned his post and sprinted towards her. He felt the strain on his aching legs immediately and his muscles were tight, but he was not going to let that prevent him from reaching her. He also knew that time was on his side, with the driver being told to delay leaving until the Police had arrived. As he tore past passengers who were both embarking and alighting the carriages, he saw her nearing the turnstile. She was walking swiftly now, almost running if her shoes had allowed it. But Robert was faster than her and as she went to go through the gate into the main station and beyond, he grabbed her arm and pulled her round. "BETTY!" he exclaimed, desperately. She turned again to face him, as did the passenger in front of her. A man with a scar across the length of his face, glanced at Robert and then briefly at Betty, and then continued on his way. Dozens of other passengers jostled to get by; frustrated by Robert and Betty blocking their exit.

Robert pulled her gently by the arm to the side of the gate to let the other passengers through as well as affording him some separate space to speak to her. "Where are you going? I told you, it wasn't what it seemed. Surely you believe me now after what we've just found? It was the young girl who dropped the brandy glasses. She must have seen something, which was why she was being chased through the dining cart. That's why she was so scared." He was desperate. Words were tumbling out of his mouth to try and impart everything that he had learned on to Betty. She looked at him with what Robert realised was pity, which he realised was not a promising sign.

She put her hand on his arm and squeezed it. "I'm flattered, Robert. Honestly, I really am. And I believe you, if that's any consolation. But this is where I get off anyway." He looked despondently at her as she continued. "You're a sweet man. Really you are. But..."

"But what?" Robert asked, hanging off her every word.

"But we're just not meant to be, that's all. It was the wrong place and the wrong time. Trust me, it's for the best. You need to go now." She went up on to her tiptoes and kissed him on the forehead. "Take care, Robert." And with that she joined the swell of passengers through the gate and away into the station. He watched her from a distance, as she left the main exit and got into the passenger seat of a car that was waiting for her, engine purring at the ready; it drove off at speed and out of sight.

He felt winded. Despite what she had said he could not help but feel that he had made a mess of the situation and his sympathy for the maid had dissipated. He resolved to find her and get to the truth of the matter and entered the train once again, making his way towards where he had left her. As he walked up the train a young woman came running through from an adjoining carriage, screaming in fear. "Murder! Murder! Fetch the Police." Robert was so wrapped up in chasing after Betty and then finding the maid that he had forgotten that nobody was guarding the end carriage. He decided to make his way there first before anyone else found Florence's body, and then deal with the maid.

"It is fine," said Robert, trying to reassure the visibly shaken woman who was fleeing in fear. He grabbed hold of her and looked sincerely into her eyes, "the Police have been sent for. Just calm down and try to forget what you saw. She's at peace now, don't worry."

The woman looked confused, alarmed even, at what Robert had said. "What do you mean *she's* at peace now?" asked the woman.

Robert continued to try and settle her, "I understand she looks a mess, but it would have been over quickly. She was stabbed in the heart." The woman looked at Robert with wide eyes filled with fear and confusion, and then took off up the carriage away from him, screaming. The poor thing, he thought to himself, must have been the shock of seeing Florence's body. The passengers in the carriage were looking at each other in alarm, and whispering to each other; clearly perturbed by the woman's behaviour and what she was saying. Their fear was allayed, however, at the sight of several Police officers running through the entrance of the station, making their way towards the train.

Robert made for the rear carriage to try and negate any further alarm, whilst all around him were now drawn to the window nearest the platform, watching Police officers yards from the train and approaching fast. Robert walked through to the carriage which contained the toilet and stopped in his tracks, frozen with shock at what he saw before him. Standing in the toilet doorway, with blood sprayed on her face and in her hair and a hairpin in her hand, stood the maid. Her face expressionless and her slender arms limp down by her side; she stared at Robert, mouth open as if all personality had drained from it. He approached her slowly, so as not to alarm her, but she stared straight through him, motionless. As he neared her, he could hear the sound of doors opening and heavy boots clattering onto the train. Police officers appeared at both ends of the carriage and stopped, as Robert leant over to her and removed the hair pin from her hand, dropping it behind him for safety. He could now see behind her into the toilet, where slumped against the seat that the maid had been sat sobbing on earlier, with his head laid against the sink facing the door was an unmistakable figure. His slick black hair was messy as if there'd been a struggle, and his expensive suit was covered in sprays of blood which also covered the walls and the floor of the toilet. He had a small puncture mark in his neck which, Robert assumed, had come from the hair pin which had been plunged into him with force by the maid. There was little doubt about her guilt; the hair pin being in her hand and the violent bursts of blood from his jugular had sprayed her, confirming her presence at the time of death.

Robert led her calmly to the awaiting Police officers, who escorted her to the rear of the train, away from the rest of the passengers who all recoiled at the horror of seeing her being led, with blood slowly dripping from her face and hair. The Conductor was at the rear of the train, informing a detective of the circumstances surrounding the discovery of Florence's death. It was left to Robert to explain the body of the cockney rogue who was laid, nearly completely exsanguinated, over the toilet sink. The Policeman was tall and thin, with a sharp, beak-like nose. He eyed the maid up and down, and then took her into the carriage which contained the body of Florence, which the conductor had covered in a blanket to spare any further alarm. He sat her down and then sat opposite her, as she stared at the floor. "What have you got to say for yourself then?" he asked her, while she continued to stare at her feet. "Hey, come on now. Silence won't help you. We've got two dead bodies here and you're covered in their blood." She looked up at him, the first response she had made since Robert had discovered her. "Why did you kill them?" He continued, undeterred by her silence, and relentless in his pursuit of a confession.

She shook her head, and frowned, almost confused by what he was saying. "No." she uttered, still shaking her head in denial. The detective looked frustrated, and shook his head at the constable who was stood next to Robert in the doorway.

"She must think I was born yesterday," he said in his deep, Cumbrian accent. "Come on now, just admit it. You're covered in blood, yes? You had the murder weapon in your hand, yes? Now how am I supposed to believe that you didn't kill the man in the toilet and this lady here?" he barked at her, pulling the blanket off Florence's body. The maid looked at the blood soaked body of her former employer and shook her head frantically, mouth open in shock. "No!" she insisted, "No! No! NO!" she cried loudly.

Robert's natural instinct was to go to her aid. Despite what she had appeared to have done, he was still pulled to her defence, suspecting that it was a crime that she had found herself committing as opposed to anything pre-planned. He sat next to her and put his arm around her for comfort and support. "Are you alright?" he asked, concerned at her mental state of mind.

The detective looked aghast at Robert. "'Are you alright', he says! Who is this idiot? Constable, get him out of here, will you. Are you alright indeed!"

The burly constable took Robert's arm and pulled him to his feet. "Come along, sir. You need to leave us to it now." He escorted a saddened Robert from the carriage as his mind tried to make sense of it all. Regardless of her guilt, the rogue that she had slain in the toilet was a rotten apple, of that he was in no doubt. Florence seemed unpleasant, but her murder had surprised him. He could not imagine the maid doing that, but then the pieces fitted. The constable left Robert to make his way back to his seat and stayed at the door to the rear carriage to ensure there were no further interruptions to proceedings, whilst the sound of the detective berating the maid echoed down the train.

Robert found himself in the dining cart to the glee of the waiter, who pounced on him before he had time to make his way through to the next compartment. "Your bill, sir!" he said, pointing at the table to Robert's left which still had the remains of his lunch that he had hoped to enjoy with Betty.

"Oh yes" said Robert solemnly, upset at the reminder. He sat at the table and stared at his chops which were now stone cold. Opposite him, Betty's plate remained with just the fat from the pork chop and some congealed gravy, thick and brown with flecks of sage running through it. Evidently the discovery of Florence's body had not deterred her from returning to the dining cart and finishing her meal. She had alerted the waiter of the issue, so that made sense. Although Robert was surprised she had an appetite after seeing such a bloody mess. She had eaten a fair amount of potatoes and vegetables too, he thought.

The bill was on a plate in the middle of the table, folded in half to conceal the total. Robert took a deep breath and opened it, baulking at the figure in the bottom right. His eyes were drawn to the top right of it though, where in different coloured ink was simply written "Sorry x". He smiled ruefully at the thought of Betty finishing her lunch, alone, while he had been babysitting a corpse, then leaving him a note to apologise. She had nothing to apologise for though, he thought to himself, regretting wasting the last of his time with her becoming embroiled in the unscrupulous developments in the rear of the train. He emptied what was left of the silver tray of vegetables and potatoes onto his plate and picked up his knife and fork to cut into one of the chops. They had been cooked perfectly; rare, just how he liked them. Despite being rested for so long, the middle of the chop still emitted a trickle of blood which stained one of the potatoes. He put the knife and fork down neatly on his plate; left the precise amount of money requested on the bill and made his way back to his seat.

The train remained at the station while the bodies were removed and blood mopped up and wiped from floors, walls, ceilings and porcelain. The new crew staff had swapped with the old, and diligently made their way from one end of the train to the other, reassuring the remaining passengers that normal service will shortly be resumed. The detective continued to direct his accusations assertively at the maid, who sat absorbing his questions like a sponge, and not giving him any answers in response. He was used to dealing with far more dangerous criminals than the fragile woman sat before him, but she was more impervious to his barrage than most he had come up against. "Have we got an identification on the bodies yet?" he asked the constable, turning his attention away from the maid who sat staring at the space previously filled by Florence's body.

"Not yet, sir, I'm afraid. No idea on the fella. All we've got on the lady is that she was called Florence." The detective stood and took a packet of cigarettes from his jacket pocket and offered one to the young girl. She shook her head at his offer, but he took one out and lit it for himself. He took a long, languid draw on it and then exhaled with a frustrated sigh; smoke filling the carriage and rising until it dispersed across the cream ceiling.

He opened a window and craned his neck to look towards the front of the train; smoke billowed from the funnel and across the tracks. He saw the body of the man being wheeled away from the station, covered in a blanket to protect the public from distress. "Right, I think we're done here Constable. We'll let these good people get on with it now. The bodies are on their way to the morgue, and you, young lady," he said, diverting his comments to the maid, "can come and assist us with our enquiries at the station."

The constable stepped towards her and took her gently by the arm; she complied with the instructions without question, as was her way. "Florence" the detective said through gritted teeth. "That's not much to go in is it? Florence what, I wonder?" His question lingered in the air, the Constable pausing at the door unable to furnish him with the answer he had asked for. The detective, not wanting to delay matters, ushered the Constable on his way with a nod of his head. But as he went to leave with the maid, she spoke for the first time with any semblance of meaning.

"Deacon" she uttered. She had only said one word consisting of two syllables; but it was information enough to pique both police officers' interest. The constable stopped, his huge, hairy hand firmly grasping her slender shoulder, as the detective looked over to her hoping for more. He was not to be disappointed, as she continued. "Her name was Florence Deacon."

Chapter Seven

Glancing around the compartment, Robert noted the familiar site of a dozing elderly lady opposite a man buried in a broadsheet. He had been as private as he could manage for the first part of the journey and after his altercation with Florence, now covered his face completely to avoid any further incident. But Robert recognised it as him due to the glare coming from his shoes and his stiff shirt cuffs. There was one notable omission, however, with Betty having been replaced by a thick set man with a thick, wiry ginger beard and dirty labourer's clothes. The contrast between the two passengers could not have been starker and Robert missed her company, her spark and her zest for life. He sat lost in thought, filtering through memories of his adulthood and regretting missed opportunities and lost love. He had to remind himself not to become too maudlin; after all, the fate of the poor maid would be the gallows, whilst the fate of her victims had already been established. One was stabbed through the heart and the other a victim of what Robert thought must have been a hideous death; violent and messy, watching his life spray from his neck, all the while knowing there was nothing that could prevent his certain death.

The train, though significantly delayed, was now across the border and into Scotland, just beyond Gretna Station, where lovers eloped to in order to take advantage of the more relaxed Scottish laws of matrimony. How ironic, Robert thought to himself briefly, before he gave himself another talking to; after all, there was no point feeling melancholy about Betty. She was quite right. Where did he think they were going to end up anyway? He would return to London, having no financial choice but to return to Simpsons, while she…well he was not sure where she was going or what she was doing. He had not thought to ask. But regardless of that, he had enjoyed their brief liaison and would take with him the lesson that opportunities should be capitalised on and not spurned and forever regretted. The old lady was quite right about that, and Robert would have told her so if she had not have been snoring so ferociously. Enough was enough, he resolved. He would put Betty to the back of his mind and just embrace whatever life threw at him from now on. He gazed over to his new travelling companion and recoiled as he picked at the inside of his nose with gusto, concentrating so hard he had his mouth open, breathing loudly and with a small amount of saliva dribbling down his chin. One thing was for sure; Robert would not be inviting him for lunch!

As they travelled across the border from Dumfriesshire into Lanarkshire, the conductor travelled once more through the train ensuring that everyone was aware of the fact that it would be splitting into two parts. Robert would travel on to Glasgow while the rear of the train made its way to Edinburgh. When the conductor entered their carriage, the old lady woke and nodded to him, smiling sweetly; the broadsheet remained unmoved in front of the gentleman, whilst the bearded fellow reacted with surprise and shot up to quickly make his way to the other end of the train, passing wind ferociously as he did so. The old lady had fallen back to sleep, the broadsheet had started to be fanned in front of the gentleman's face, whilst Robert was left gagging on the sulphuric smell that he had left to fill the compartment. He opened a window to let some fresh air in, and stood breathing in the Scottish air by the lungful. The train ground slowly to a halt and the crew began splitting the train, whilst Robert stood thinking about the future. He was now in a different country, and was nearing an end to this particular journey. Although what the next two days had in store was unlikely to come close to what he had gone through in the last few hours.

As he stared at the sky, clouds had gathered above and were filled with an angry looking blackness that certainly threatened rain at the very least, and the light had dimmed in the compartment itself. The sound of snoring continued, with just the ruffle of newspaper pages to accompany it. When Betty entered his head briefly, he decided a change of scenery was required to perk him up; so off to the dining cart he went in order to find some liquid refreshment.

The train pulled away and began its journey into the Valley of Clyde, while Robert sat alone drinking, albeit in a more measured, methodical manner than he had done earlier with Betty. They travelled at pace through the coal mining districts of Lanarkshire and the steel works of Motherwell and Newton, until at last at six forty-five pm the train pulled up at Glasgow Central station, a mere fifty minutes late. They had been travelling for eight and three quarter hours, had crossed a dozen county borders and had played host to two murders.

He stood and stretched, having spent the final hour at the table drinking beer, the speed at which increasing the more he drank. His legs were stiff from his recent inertia after the exercise that he had had earlier on, both sprinting for the train as well as after Betty. As people started to depart the train, he made for the exit and then realised with horror that he had left his luggage in the compartment, so once again found himself sprinting through carriages and cursing his forgetfulness. By the time that he had got to the front carriage, it was empty except for his luggage that was safely stored away above his seat. The old lady had evidently woken, or been woken by someone else, and had gone on her way to visit the family of which she was so proud of. Whilst the gentleman had disappeared, taking with him whatever secret he had managed to keep from all except for Florence.

Leaving the train and patting his jacket pocket to feel the reassuring presence of his wallet and paperwork, he made his way to the exit as people flitted about in front of him, meeting and greeting and rushing off to enjoy their evenings. The light was now distinctly gloomy and rain began to fall, gently at first, but then much heavier until everybody rushed for the shelter of the main body of the station; Robert included.

Stood amidst a swell of people in the station, the rain poured from the sky as though a pipe had suddenly burst without warning, soaking everything it hit in an instant. The majority stayed under cover, despite the deafening noise of the deluge of rain hitting the glass ceiling. Whilst those lucky enough to have transport waiting for them braved the first few yards from the exit until safely within their vehicle, suffering only collateral water damage to their clothes and hair. Robert took his paperwork from his pocket and read once more the instructions within the letter, which confirmed that he would be picked up by car. He had noticed cars outside, many of which had already departed, so he fought his way through the crowd to the main exit. The light outside was now exceptionally dark, so visibility was poor. He was unclear if it was due to the night drawing in or just the sheer volume of dark clouds above, but either way he could not see anything obviously waiting for him so he decided to stay dry for a little while longer.

He looked around the waiting area to see if he recognised anyone, but failing to do so, he resumed his solitude and continued with his own thoughts; a circumstance in which he had become accustomed. He leant against the wall to take the pressure off his legs a little, with thoughts of what could possibly lie ahead and why he had even been invited. He did not regret accepting the invitation though, focusing on his new raison d'etre; to capitalise on opportunities that were presented to him. So deep were his thoughts, that he had entirely missed the fact that the rain had now stopped and people had begun to file out of the exit. It was only when he noticed that the peripheral noise of chatter, laughter and rain beating down on the roof had ceased, that he realised he was stood alone with the exception of railway staff and the odd passenger arriving for the next train departing from Glasgow.

He once again made his way over to the main exit, passing through the ornate, green and gold painted iron doors onto the Gordon Street pavement. He sought to fill his lungs with fresh Scottish air, but instead was subjected to second hand cigarette smoke which closely resembled wet hay and cow dung. Looking over to where the smell seemed to be emanating from, he saw two men standing in front of their cars, absolutely sodden with rain which still dripped from the end of their noses. They were holding a piece of card each. The writing on them barely legible; so smeared were they from the violent downpour. He approached the first man and put his head to within inches of the sign, while the man eyed him, barely even acknowledging Robert's approach. He just about made out the writing, which spelt out the name, Mrs F Deacon. He then turned his attention to the second driver, a wizened man who appeared to be the culprit who was creating the foul aroma from his hand rolled cigarette that hung out of his mouth. Squinting to read his sign, he made out the name, Mr R Johnson. "Ah, you must be my driver. I'm Robert Johnson. Is this your car behind you then?"

The driver, expressionless, eyed Robert plainly, whilst rain still slowly ran down his face. "Aye. You took ya time" he replied, clearly unhappy at being stood under the downpour waiting for him while Robert remained dry inside the station. "I don't suppose you had a Mrs Deacon in there with ya, keeping dry?"

Robert felt guilty at how wet the two drivers were, although he was a little unsure why they could not have just sat in their cars, but dare not mention it. "I'm sorry," Robert replied, "I've no idea who she is, other than I recognise the surname. Perhaps she'll be on a different train?" The other driver muttered something under his breath, but Robert thought better of asking him to repeat it. "So, is this your car then?" Robert asked, trying to move things along.

"Aye" replied the driver as he opened the back door for Robert, then got himself ready in the driver's seat. Robert put his luggage on the seat next to him, patted his jacket to check the contents, once again, and then shut the door. At that the driver pulled away, leaving his compatriot fruitlessly waiting alone for his passenger, whose body was in the process of being transported to the local morgue.

Robert tried to get comfortable in the back of the car, but it was old and well-used and the seat was hard and lumpy beneath him. "How long until we get to where we're going then?" Robert asked, keen to know the length of time he would have to endure.

"Long enough," came the reply from the man of seemingly few words.

"I'm only asking because I need to spend a penny. I had a few beers on the way, you see" Robert said, as the driver muttered something under his breath. "I beg your pardon, I didn't catch that?" Robert asked.

"I said ya late enough as it is. All the others left aboot half an hour afore."

"What others?" asked Robert, confused.

"The others from the train heading for Knoydart, they all had their own cars. And they are about thirty miles ahead o' ya." At this Robert kicked himself; if only he had seen the driver straight away, he could have had a glimpse of who else was invited.

"I'm dreadfully sorry, but I really do need to go. I don't suppose you could pull over for a second, could you?" The driver cursed under his breath, and pulled left sharply at the side of the road.

"Reet. Hurry up aboot ya. I have nae got all neet" he snapped, shaking his head in frustration.

While Robert relieved himself at the side of the road, the driver rolled himself another cigarette and lit it just as Robert got back into the car. "Interesting aroma, what brand is it?" he asked, coughing at the first sign of smoke wafting over the seats towards the rear of the car.

"Willie from ma village makes it himsel'. Don't ask me, I get it cos it's the cheapest." The car pulled away once more, heading north.

"It's getting chilly" Robert said, shivering and pulling his jacket around himself.

The driver, sat in a thick wool-lined jacket with gloves on to protect himself from the cold, smirked. "Aye," he replied, "that it is."

"You mentioned a place that we're heading to?" asked Robert, "What did you say it was called?"

The driver, glanced at Robert through the rear view mirror and replied, "Knoydart." The conversation was getting tediously one-sided, but Robert continued to pursue more details.

"So how far away is it? I've never heard of it?" The driver puffed at his cigarette, causing foul-smelling acrid smoke to fill the car once again.

"I'd settle doon and get some sleep if I were ya. You've got a fair few hours yet." This news was not welcome as far as Robert was concerned, and there was very little chance of sleep in such an uncomfortable car.

Robert noticed that the driver had started chuckling to himself, which was the first time his pock-marked face had pulled much of an expression other than a surly scowl or a sarcastic smirk. "What's so funny?" asked Robert, trying hard not to sound irked, despite suspecting that the laughter was at his expense somehow.

"If ye'r cold noo, ya wait till you get on the boot?" he chuckled.

"The boot?" Robert asked, confused once again.

"Aye," the driver replied, "the boot", laughing now, rather than chuckling.

"The boot?" wondered Robert, until realising. "Oh! The boat. Hang on a minute, what boat?"

The driver continued to laugh, "Yooz got two choices. The boot, or the road, an I'm not tekin' my car on that road. I'll teck you as far as I can, and that's as far as the boot." Smoke had now completely filled the car, so the driver opened his window, which served to clear the car of smoke, although not the stench, but also make it even colder.

"But it's pitch black already and it's started to rain again. Isn't a boat going to be dangerous?" asked Robert with concern.

The driver eyed him in the mirror again; "Aye!"

Chapter Eight

The journey from Glasgow to Knoydart was exactly one hundred miles, and Robert estimated that they had travelled about half of them. He had managed to extract the distance from the driver after several attempts, and after another comfort break that was where their conversation had ended. The driver, it had been disclosed, was concerned about not being paid if he did not deliver Robert on time. So Robert had agreed to let him concentrate solely on driving and to avoid any further delays.

As the car continued on its long journey, Robert had pulled the lapels from his jacket up against the bottom of his face and tried to huddle up to conserve some warmth. He turned sideways and despite the discomfort, leant his head against the back seat to rest it. Staring out of the window revealed no clues as to where he was or where he was going. The darkness had rendered him quite blind to anything outside of the car; all he could see was the faint outline of his own reflection. Whilst inside the car he could only make out the intermittent orange glow of the putrid cigarette that the sullen driver would suck on occasionally. He thought about the farcical toing and froing in the office with Arthur and Jim which seemed an eternity ago. It seemed incomprehensible that it had occurred on this very day; the light-hearted prelude to the devastating turn of events that had proceeded. He caught sight of his own reflection which revealed a broad grin, brought about by replaying Arthur bumbling about in the office with his hand covering his mouth and nose to protect him from the germs from Robert's faux-illness. He began to replay the subsequent events of the day to himself, which gave his reflection a more sombre appearance. While he daydreamed, the low rattle from the car's engine had evolved into a distant white noise. He blinked slowly and thought of Betty. He imagined her next to him in the car and pulled his arms around his torso for warmth and pictured wrapping himself around her to share their body heat; the excitement of the thought made him oblivious to the ever decreasing temperature. He blocked out the blood, the chaos and the tears; he had seen enough of that to last him several lifetimes, and focused on happier thoughts. He remembered her on tip toes, leaning up to his face and kissing him on the forehead. He smiled once more and imagined her deep brown eyes, shining and sparkling for him. Never mind that it was the wrong time and the wrong place; these were happy thoughts and soothed him as, in spite of his discomfort, he drifted slowly to sleep.

The pleasant thoughts that he had before succumbing to tiredness had been replaced by a jumbled mess of nonsense; dining on a train journey with Thomas Deacon, who was drinking sheep's blood, to the horror of the other passengers. He was gulping it as though he had been denied refreshment for days and it spilled from the sides of his mouth and ended up all over his shirt. A woman screamed in horror and ran through the dining cart, warning the other passengers of a murderer being on board. Arthur was there too, shielding his mouth with his hand and recoiling at the sight of Deacon who continued to quaff glass after glass of blood, refilled for him by Claude, the waiter. Robert sat opposite and could not avert his eyes from Deacon, who eventually put the glass down and wiped his mouth with the back of his hand; smearing the cold blood across his face as he did so. He smiled, his teeth imbrued with blood and his eyes wild, then stood and leant over Robert who could smell his breath which reeked of tobacco and carrion. He leant closer, inches away from Robert who sat trapped, unable to move, unable to scream for help. "It's time to go" he said, his face twisted into a hideous mixture of delight and lunacy. "Well? What are you waiting for? I said what are you waiting for?" Deacon's voice did not sound right; he was not Scottish! Robert's confusion turned to horror as Deacon's bloody hands grabbed him by his lapels and shook him and shouted "Git yoursel' oot a ma car, man!"

Robert jumped awake and put his hands up in defence against his assailant. His eyes were bleary and he could not focus immediately, made worse by the blinding darkness that enveloped him. The breath against him was stale and unpleasant, but familiar to him, and after the initial shock he was relieved when his eyes adjusted to make out the face of his driver. "I said come on with ya. I have to get back home and get some kip me sen ya kin." Robert opened his mouth to speak but found his mouth virtually stuck together after having nothing to drink since beer on the train approximately six hours earlier. His mouth tasted nearly as bad as the driver's breath smelt; what he would give for some cold water.

He shifted in his seat to try and get out of the car, but the extreme dull ache in his hip prevented him from moving immediately. The driver pinched the bridge of his nose in frustration and stamped his right foot. "Please Mister. The boot's all ready for ya. Come on noo. Hurry up oot o' ma car."

Robert slid himself out of the car and straightened himself up into a standing position. He stretched and as he did so his back clicked and the muscles in his neck and shoulders pulled painfully. "Thank you" he said, "do I owe you anything?"

The driver, having already slammed the back door and ran round the car to get back into his seat, paused "Och, no! That's all tecken care of. Duncan will teck you from here. Good luck!" he smirked, "you'll be needing it!" At which he started the car up and sped off into the night, leaving Robert next to a small fishing boat upon which stood a large set man, who looked just as irritated at Robert as the driver had at the train station.

The man looked Robert up and down and looked suitably unimpressed. At that, Robert leant against the side of the boat and put one foot on board, causing it to move slightly which resulted in him doing the splits. His left foot was on the ground, his right on the boat and the rest of his body hovered over the dark, murky water below. As a sharp pain soared up the insides of his leg and into his groin, a strong arm grabbed him under his armpit and in one swift movement, hoisted him safely aboard.

"Thank you", Robert said, embarrassed at the scene he was making. His new companion looked at him with disdain and made his way to the cabin to begin the journey to Knoydart. Robert sat to compose himself and leant his hand against the edge of the small vessel. As well as the shock of the cold dampness on his skin, he was surprised to feel that it was made from metal. He imagined initially that it was going to be a rickety, wooden boat, but it seemed far larger and more robust than he had feared, which pleased him. Despite this, however, there was still an element of danger which emanated inside him; borne out of the hour, the mode of transport, the harsh rain which continued to beat down on him, the nature of his journey and the events of the day. Despite the fact it seemed slightly safer than what he had expected, he was being taken by boat, sailed by a total stranger in the middle of the night, in a storm to who knows where for who knows what reason. These facts would normally be cause for concern for him, but he felt almost powerless to worry himself about it and adopted a surprisingly un-Robert-like laissez-faire attitude towards the man who he was entrusting his life to.

The dampness from the wooden benching on the edge of the boat had begun to seep through Robert's trousers and made his skin even more wet and cold. He had initially decided to sit separately from the sailor, but looking at him enclosed inside the wooden cabin from where he steered the vessel, he decided that joining him inside was marginally more attractive than catching pneumonia. He tried to open the door, pulling at the handle but without success. The sailor laughed at Robert, who was now stood looking into the dry cabin whilst being rained on from above. "It's not locked, son!" the sailor reassured him, "use a bit of strength!" He grabbed the handle and pulled, but only the top part of the door made any sort of movement, opening a fraction, with the lower half still shut firmly. The sailor shook his head and chuckled, putting Robert out of his misery by shoving the door open with a single barge of his shoulder. "Told you" he said, and then roared with laughter. "It always does that in damp weather. Which means it always does that!" he laughed again in a deep guttural manner.

Robert felt useless and pitiful, but also relieved as the mood of the man had clearly lifted since their departure; probably out of pity, he thought to himself. The engine of the boat hummed steadily and they made fairly steady progress across the water towards Knoydart. The sailor pulled the door back shut which produced a cold waft of air, hitting Robert and causing him to shiver. It was freezing, he was soaking wet and he was completely inappropriately dressed, having underestimated the stark contrast in conditions compared to London. The sailor, noting Robert's reaction, picked up a bottle of whisky and offered it to him. Robert hesitated; his body needed water not more alcohol, although he was instinctively tempted. "Go on, it'll do you good" the sailor insisted. Robert took the bottle, unscrewed the cap and wiped the rim of the bottle on the arm of his jacket, to which the sailor looked perplexed. He then took a long swig. The sailor laughed his deep, throaty laugh again. "Better?"

Robert nodded confirmation. "Better."

"Good!" said the sailor, taking the bottle and putting it back on the side. "I'm Duncan" he said, holding out his hand towards Robert. Robert took it and shook, then winced in pain. The grip of his hand was vice-like and the coarse callouses on his palm dug into Robert's. He noticed Robert's discomfort and laughed once again at his predicament.

"I know who you are, so don't worry about introducing yourself. So what took you, Robert? The others are all tucked up in bed by now, or having a nightcap in front of the fire!" The very thought of which made Robert yearn for warmth and comfort, two feelings that he had been denied for a great many hours.

"I missed my lift" answered Robert. "It was raining hard as I got off the train, so I sheltered in the station until it had passed." The sailor looked at Robert plainly then roared with laughter again, irritating him slightly as it was inevitably at Robert's expense. "What's so funny?" he asked.

"You missed your lift because you were keeping dry, you say?" Duncan asked, to which Robert nodded. He looked at Robert, who was sat shivering and soaking wet, "Well a fat lot of good that did you!" He roared once more and turned to switch his attention to plotting his course to Knoydart.

"You don't sound very Scottish" Robert remarked. "With a name like Duncan, I expected an accent to accompany it."

"That's because I'm not" he replied. "My Father was, hence the name, but my mother is from London. I was brought up there, hence the accent that I do have."

"So what brings you up here in the middle of the night ferrying me over the water?" Robert enquired. He was keen to keep things as friendly as possible.

Duncan looked at Robert, as though he was pondering on an answer. "The fishing!" he replied, "It's in the blood! There's nothing that beats a life on the sea," he continued, pausing only to hand the whisky back to Robert. "The freedom; the tranquillity, the fact that I'm my own boss and then the thrill of the catch. It's all nets these days, but I still cast a rod over the side on a fine day. Do you fish, Robert?" he asked, to which Robert gave a definite shake of the head, whilst cradling the whisky bottle between his hands. He was tired and cold and now only wanted a bed in which to sleep. "We'll be there soon, son" he said, almost reading Robert's mind. "It's a shame you don't fish though. You need patience to make a catch; and I have patience. Oh yes. I'll wait as long as it takes. I'll tease and tempt and let it think that there's no danger and all is safe and well, as it nibbles at the bait that I've offered it. I'll sit and I'll watch, toying with it as it takes its fill. Then when it least expects it, and it's at its most relaxed, I'll pull and I'll wind it slowly towards me, giving a little as it struggles before I wind it in again. I'll let it struggle, easing a little every now and then, letting it think it's getting away until it tires of struggling and has nothing left to offer. Then I'll make my move and reel it in completely until it's fighting for its life between my hands right here on this very boat. Then I put it out of its misery, with a short, sharp knock to the head.

"What's wrong, Robert? You look a little green around the gills. Will you have another drink?" he said, still looking at him, with one hand on the wheel and the other hanging by his side.

"I think I've had enough." Robert replied, suddenly feeling very uneasy. He looked down at the whisky suspiciously, as silence filled the inside of the cabin, with just the peripheral sound of water lapping at the boat and of rain pounding the cabin roof. Duncan took a step towards Robert, letting go of the wheel which span, turning the boat from right to left. He leant out his huge right hand, making Robert flinch backwards, and in one swift motion plucked the bottle from his hand and sank what was left in one. He winked at Robert, chuckled to himself and then turned his attention to realigning their path. "Don't worry son, I'm only playing with you!" he said, "Not long now and we'll be there. Then you can get that sleep you've been hankering after."

Whilst ultimately relived that Duncan posed no threat after all, he could have done without the unnecessary jocularity and his heart was positively racing. He had had his fill of drama for one day, but he thought it best not to mention it, settling on silently, sailing his way to what he hoped would be a swift resolution to his fatigue. He was not to be disappointed, as for the rest of the journey Duncan pressed ahead, diverting his attention just once in order to open another bottle of whisky for himself. He had a half empty crate of them by his feet with another sealed one next to it. Clearly drinking whisky was an essential requirement to life at sea. Resuming his drinking had made Duncan whistle. The tune was unfamiliar to Robert, but it was bright and jolly; a complete juxtaposition to how Robert was feeling.

Ten minutes and approximately twenty five centilitres of whisky later, Duncan slowed the boat down and gently eased it next to the shore with expert precision which belied his alcohol consumption. "There we go young Robert. Your carriage awaits you" he said laughing to himself once again. Robert had given up trying to rationalise what made everything so funny the moment he saw how much he drank. But the carriage that he referred to was not part of his metaphorical ramblings; it was in fact parked about fifty yards from the boat. Not a carriage as such, but a car in which sat the silhouetted figure of a man who had started the engine as the boat came into view. "Well what are you waiting for, young Robert. Off you go. Unless you want to keep me company on the way back" Duncan chuckled in his trademark manner.

"No, you've done enough," Robert replied, "I'm grateful you hang on for me, especially in this weather."

"Ha! This is nothing. It's positively balmy," Duncan said before unleashing his laugh again. "Now off you go, and Robert...." he stared intently in his eyes and gripped his hand firmly. "Look after yourself, won't you." Robert nodded as Duncan continued to hold his hand and look at him, almost transfixed. Before suddenly snapping out of his trance-like state and becoming the jocular, huge personality that Robert had become accustomed to on their journey. "Well go on then. Bugger off!" he said, winking.

Robert was relieved to have land beneath his feet, albeit ground that had been turned almost bog-like by the incessant cascade of water that continued to beat its way down from the black skies above. It seemed to be getting heavier and showed no sign of stopping; Robert's clothes were now absolutely wet through, as though he had just bathed fully dressed. He trudged his way as fast as he could towards the waiting car, already dreading the inevitable mess he was going to make in the footwell of the passenger seat. With each step, his shoes, socks and the bottom of his trouser legs became caked in thick clay-like mud. He resolved to sit in the back to hide the inevitable mess, having already put everyone to additional inconvenience due to his earlier tardiness.

He finally reached the end of the sodden ground and the few yards between himself and the awaiting car was almost gravel-like. Robert did his best to scrape as much mud from his shoes on the rough ground as he could, but other than the larger lumps of excess which were removed fairly easily, the remainder stuck to his shoes, impervious to any remedial efforts to remove it. The engine of the car continued to run, emitting a low steady hum; exhaust fumes slowly seeping from the rear of the vehicle and rising briefly before the wind dissipated it. The driver remained unmoved and stared out of the windscreen ahead into the darkness, with his side profile being only partially visible to Robert.

Having done as much as he could to clean himself up he approached the car as swiftly as he could in order to escape from the harsh conditions. The wind had picked up which meant the rain was now almost horizontal and lashed at his face, so the awaiting car offered shelter at the very least. He pulled open the rear passenger side door, put his luggage in the footwell behind the driver's seat and then gingerly sat down, shutting the door behind him just as the wind threatened to slam it for him. The driver turned to face him and smiled. "Welcome, Mr Johnson. My name is Harold; I'm here to take you to the Manor House. I trust you've had a comfortable and pleasant trip so far?" he enquired, amiably.

Robert, muscles aching, cold to the bone, dripping wet and having endured a murderous nearly nine hour train journey, which was merely a prelude to his car and boat journeys, was unsure whether the question was in fact an attempt at levity. But by the pleasant demeanour on Harold's face, Robert decided it was the automatic conversation starter from a man in service, and so deserved a suitable response. "It's been fine, Harold, thank you. But I'm looking forward to it reaching its conclusion fairly soon. Please tell me the Manor House is nearby?"

"It's not too far at all, Mr Johnson. We'll be there in about five or ten minutes" Harold replied with a reassuring smile.

"Thank God!" Robert sighed in relief, "I was starting to think I'd never make it here."

"Well you're here now, sir" Harold replied, and then turned back to face the road ahead whilst slowly the car began its short journey to the Manor House.

Chapter Nine

The car pulled up directly outside the front door of the Manor House. From where he sat he could see that it was a large, imposing building but that was as much as he could tell. Robert had no idea what hour it was but it was still pitch black and the rain still fell heavily. Harold had the good sense to be wearing a large, heavy looking rain coat which was buttoned up and offered him at least a modicum of protection.

As he opened the door for Robert, Harold's eyes were immediately drawn to the state of both Robert's lower half and the seat and floor of the car. "Sorry about that," Robert said, "I tried to get it off but…"

"Think nothing of it, sir" Harold replied. "I'll clean it up in the morning. Get yourself in the warm, sir and take those muddy shoes off. I'll fetch you something to change into."

The door was plain, except for a large metal knocker and a large round metal handle. It looked sturdy and Robert could tell it was heavy by the way that Harold opened it. At least they would all be safe and secure this evening, he thought to himself, as Harold bolted it shut. "If you take those shoes off sir, I'll get them cleaned up for you so they're ready for the morning." Robert removed them carefully, trying not to flick mud anywhere in addition to where he had stepped already.

"It really is beastly out there isn't it?" Harold asked rhetorically. "It hasn't been this bad for some time."

"Just my luck, eh? Forgive me but where am I sleeping?" was all that Robert could muster in terms of a response amidst his tiredness.

"All in good time, sir" Harold replied. "Let's get you out of those wet clothes first. You'll catch your death!"

"Really I'm fine. I'd much rather just get to bed, if it's all the same with you" countered Robert, fruitlessly.

"Nonsense, sir", Harold insisted. "Come this way."

Robert reluctantly followed Harold along the hallway, lit merely by candles, until they reached the dining room. They had already passed two other rooms, the contents of which were unknown to Robert as each door was shut. Harold opened the door and Robert followed him in to the room that was already lit and a welcoming fire was burning at the far end. Perhaps warming himself up first would be a more prudent idea than getting into bed soaked to the skin, he thought to himself. He made his way over where great warmth was emanating from, and stood as near as he could manage in order to provide some welcome relief to the harsh conditions that he had encountered since arriving in Glasgow.

He turned to give his back some warmth to find that Harold had already left, leaving Robert alone. Glancing around the large room it was immediately obvious that there were a number of guests already in situ. The large oval dining table was laid for what looked like about ten people, there was a sideboard on the wall opposite where Robert stood and he could see what looked like an array of different spirits in decanters on top of it. His body had started to feel warmth at his core such was the heat from the fire, so Robert decided to have a small medicinal tipple to help him sleep. He opened one of the doors of the sideboard and found a shelf full of glasses; scanning it quickly, he opted for a large brandy glass. As he shut the door he noticed that the sideboard was quite dusty, which would not normally have bothered him, particularly as his own house was far from pristine. But he found it odd that a grand old house like this would be dusty; after all, Harold was in service here, and Robert had assumed there would be other staff.

He poured himself a large brandy from the grand-looking decanter, and took a sip in order to savour the taste. Whilst he was no expert on the subject, he was, however, a seasoned drinker and the brandy tasted decidedly odd. There was nothing wrong with it per se, but having expected a fine, delicate taste; it almost tasted like a cheap bottle one might find in a public house. He suddenly became conscious that he was unfairly judging the quality of someone else's drink that he was helping himself to and admonished himself. Disappointment notwithstanding, he drank the brandy back in one go just as Harold came back into the room. The aftertaste was harsh and the back of his throat burned, which made Robert cough.

"I see you've found the refreshments, sir?" Harold remarked.

"I'm sorry, "spluttered Robert, "I thought it would do me good."

"Naturally, sir. Let me pour you another" Harold replied, laying the clothes he had in his hands over the back of one of the dining chairs and picking the decanter up.

"No! Robert insisted, putting his hand on Harold's to prevent him from refilling the glass, "really it's fine."

"Right you are sir. I was just informing chef of your arrival so that your meal can be prepared. And here are some fresh clothes, sir."

"Oh God no!" said Robert, almost in shock. "Don't disturb him at this hour, I'm fine, really."

"It's really no bother, Sir" Harold insisted. "Once chef learnt of your delay they absolutely insisted that I inform them of your arrival. Chef was adamant, sir. Chef said that it would warm you up, sir."

"Well that's very kind of him," said Robert, "but I really don't want to put him out."

"It's already done, sir. Chef's just adding the finishing touches to it. Now while you're waiting I'll leave you to it. If you get yourself changed into these fresh clothes, once I serve you your meal I can take your clothes away and get them laundered for you, sir."

It was clear to Robert that Harold was not going to take no for an answer, and given that he had no idea where he was sleeping, he agreed to his kind offer. "Right ho" said Robert. "You win. I guess a warm meal and fresh clothes would be best."

"Very good, sir" Harold replied with a smile and a nod of the head. "I'll just go and fetch your meal while you change. Don't worry, sir. You won't be disturbed." And with that Robert once again found himself alone in the dining room. He undressed with difficulty in front of the fire to keep as warm as possible, his heavy, soaking wet clothes sticking to him. Once he had managed to remove them all he stood naked to try and dry his skin and rubbed his arms and legs to try and speed the process up. He looked at his genitals which were a sorry sight, having shrivelled up to virtually nothing because of the cold; he held them in his right hand and shook at them to try and revive them back into life. But as he did so a sound came from behind him. He spun round in alarm to see that the room was in fact empty, but in doing so he noticed that the curtains were open in front of the nearest of the three windows.

He approached the window gingerly, still cupping his genitals in his hand. Pressing his nose against the pane, he looked out expecting to see someone on the other side of the glass. But reassuringly, other than the tired, bedraggled image of his own reflection he could see nothing other than rain running down the glass. He turned to go back to the fire to finish dressing as the door opened and Harold entered the room. Robert gasped in horror and placed his left hand over his genitals too, as though the second hand would afford him more protection and make him less naked somehow. Harold, however, acted oblivious to Robert's position and continued as though everything was perfectly normal.

"Here we are sir, your meal" Harold said, placing the offering at the place nearest the fire. I'll put you here, sir, so that you can continue to warm yourself. Once I informed chef of the dreadful state you'd arrived in there was great degree of satisfaction in having cooked this particular meal for you, sir. Guaranteed to warm you up, chef says, sir."

"Well," Robert said, still cupping his modesty with both hands, "make sure you thank chef very much from me, won't you. I'm honoured that he prepared this with me in mind."

"I will do in the morning, sir" Harold replied. "Chef left for bed as soon as the dish was served as breakfast is served soon." Robert felt guilty on hearing this, so many people being put out by his stupidity. Harold, sensing Robert's reaction, reassured him. "Don't worry, sir. We've had later nights than tonight. I can assure you. Now let's sort these wet clothes out shall we, sir?"

"Of course, yes" replied Robert, keen not to hold Harold up any further, realising that he too would be required on duty very soon for breakfast. Harold picked up the sodden clothes while

Robert walked over towards the food. All of a sudden a powerful aroma hit Robert's nose; the waft of which was emanating from the plate that had suddenly raised his interest levels. He looked at it with great curiosity and saw what looked like a vibrant stew, with hunks of charred meat within the thick red sauce. Next to this was a small bowl with white sauce in with small green things stirred into it and on a separate smaller plate was something that Robert had never seen before; he stared at it trying to make out what it was.

"It's bread, sir" Harold said, perceptively reading Robert's confused gaze.

"Bread?" Robert replied, "It's like no bread I've ever seen before. It's perfectly flat with blackened bubbles all over it. And what is this exactly?" he asked, nodding towards the red stew, "I've never smelt anything like it."

"That is achar gosht, sir" Harold replied.

"I beg your pardon?" said Robert, raising one eyebrow and cocking his ear towards Harold as if he had literally misheard him.

"Achar gosht, sir." Harold confirmed to the unmoved Robert. "It's a hot and sour lamb curry."

"Curry!" Robert exclaimed, "My word. I've heard of it but never tried it. So that's what it smells like then?" he replied, salivating at the thought of it, and breathing the aroma in deeply. He then smelt at the white substance in the small bowl.

"That's mint yoghurt, sir" Harold informed him. "Chef wasn't sure how adventurous you were, so that's there just in case. It will soothe your mouth if the curry is too highly spiced for your palate. I'll leave you to your meal, sir. These clothes will be ready for you in the morning."

"I can't thank you enough, Harold. For everything I mean." Harold looked at Robert, smiled and silently nodded. "I can't help but think we've met before though. You seem familiar."

"I don't think so, sir" replied Harold. "I can't imagine how we would have done."

"No I guess not," said Robert. "Anyway, never mind that. I don't want to hold you up any further, Harold."

"Of course, sir. Oh and if you don't mind, chef recommended this to accompany your meal." Harold said, indicating with his open hand a glass of amber coloured liquid which was unmistakably ale.

"Thank you, Harold. My reputation must go before me, clearly."

"Yes, sir, I'm sure. I'll return shortly to show you to your room" replied Harold, and turned and departed the room, leaving Robert to dress and eat. With the door shut, Robert picked up the clothes which had been laid over the back of the chair all this time. He had not noticed them in any detail as his attention had been focused on preserving his modesty before being completely distracted by the exotic aroma of the meal that he had been served. He picked up a white shirt, and hurriedly buttoned it up before picking up a caramel coloured pair of trousers which he put on to enable him to finally sit down to eat. He picked up a fork and raised a piece of meat to his mouth, examining it briefly before placing it on his tongue. The meat was charred and gnarly around the edges and was covered in delightful looking gravy. The immediate sensation exploded on his tongue with tastes that he had never experienced before, followed by a wave of new flavours, coming at him in layers. It really was the finest thing that he had ever tried. He was not even hungry but suddenly found himself devouring every mouthful. He was less keen on the white sauce, but found it cooling as every now and then one particular mouthful seemed hotter than before. But before long he had polished off the entire plateful, and mopped up the gravy with the bread.

He sat back in the chair, exhausted but full and content, and then slowly drank the ale that had been left to accompany the meal. At this point Harold entered the room again and before he had a chance to ask if the meal was satisfactory, Robert was already answering him! "Who is this chef, Harold? I've never in my life tasted anything like this. He's a genius."

Harold gave Robert a wry smile, "Chef will be delighted, sir. Now if you're ready, I'll show you to your room. Let's get you some shut eye, shall we?"

"Of course, of course. Let's go" Robert replied, as both men left the room, Robert following Harold bare-footed from the dining room. He was led along the remainder of the hallway before ascending the wide wooden stairs. The walls up the staircase were filled with portraits of people that Robert assumed were connected with the house; old men, young women, a woman seated with a man stood behind her with his hand on her shoulder and a satisfied look on his face almost saying 'look at what I've got'. Each one looked older than the previous one, the subjects and artists were presumably long since dead.

As they arrived at the top of the stairs, the rooms spread out from right to left and Robert could hear the faint noise of snoring coming from at least one of them. Harold stopped near the end of the corridor and opened the door to Robert's room. It already had a candle glowing in it and a fire had been lit some time ago, which had resulted in a warm, welcoming room. There were towels on the end of what looked a very inviting, freshly laundered bed. "Hopefully this should suffice, sir. You have towels here for your ablutions; the bathroom is the room at the end, two doors down. Breakfast is served at eight am, which is in about three hours' time, sir."

Robert grimaced at this news, "thank you, Harold. You've been such a help."

"It's been a pleasure, sir. Goodnight" Harold replied, and closed the door as he backed out of the room.

Robert took the trousers and shirt off and laid them over the end of the bed. He pulled the tightly stretched blankets away from the soft sheet and climbed inside, pulling the blankets back up to just below his chin. He lay with his eyes tightly shut and could hear the distant sounds of Harold clearing up plates, which were soon followed by the sound of his footsteps as he made his way to bed himself. Robert had fantasised about this moment and imagined immediate sleep, but to his frustration he was still awake. The events of the day replayed themselves in his head, although not in chronological order, but more of a jumbled up affair. As he lay there his chest became tight and a dull ache resonated in his ribcage which he did his best to ignore. His heart pumped faster than was normal whilst laid down, which he reasoned was due to the adrenaline that had been coursing through his body. The effect of this made his head pulse uncontrollably like the beat from a drum being thumped. He tried his best to ignore his body, unsuccessfully at first, but before too long, thankfully, he had drifted off into a long overdue sleep.

Chapter Ten

Robert woke and immediately cursed himself for not urinating before going to sleep. His bladder had once again got the better of him and despite trying to ignore it and put himself back to sleep, it was no use. He got up and immediately felt disorientated, fumbling around at the foot of the bed in order to find his trousers. Having successfully located them and put them on, just in case, he made his way to the toilet. He did not mind being caught topless, but after the shenanigans in the dining room with Harold, he wanted to avoid any repetition, especially with the likelihood of there being female guests. He left his room and quietly shut the door, then made his way to the last room of the corridor. Fortunately, or unfortunately as the case may be, light was just beginning to break outside and gave enough visibility in the bathroom for him to locate the toilet and washing facilities. Having successfully emptied his bladder he made his way back, shutting the bathroom door quietly and entering the room next door. The room was pitch black, thanks to the curtains protecting his sore eyes from the imminent daylight. Something was not right though and in his tired, confused state he could not make out what it was. The room was freezing, he realised; the fire must have gone out without him realising. He made his way over to the bed and once again was confused; the bed was bare, no blankets, pillows with no covers on and the mattress was cold to the touch. He stood trying to understand what was happening, when the door opened slowly, and the familiar figure of Harold entered the room.

"Can I help you, sir?" he enquired.

"Someone's put my fire out and taken my bed clothes, Harold" replied Robert. His voice croaky from tiredness as well as the dryness caused by the curry he had eaten before retiring.

"This is not your room, sir. Your room is next door."

"Oh God! Harold, I'm so sorry! I didn't realise. I'm so sorry" Robert said, wracked in guilt at having disturbed Harold once again through sheer foolishness.

"No harm done, sir. I was on my way to help chef and heard a noise. I just wanted to check if everything was okay."

"Yes. Yes" Robert reassured him. "I just needed the toilet and must have come back to the wrong room. I'll get dressed for breakfast and come down."

"No need, sir" Harold said, "It's only six thirty; you have an hour and a half to get a bit more sleep. I'll see you to your room."

"It's fine, Harold. I can make my own way next door! Who's room is this then?" asked Robert.

"This room belongs to Mrs Deacon, sir?"

"Oh. Is she not here then?" asked Robert.

"I believe she's been delayed, sir. Shall we go, sir?" asked Harold, trying to remove Robert from the room.

Robert entered his own room to the reassuring glow of fire embers which still ensured the room had sufficient warmth. He climbed back into bed and pulled his knees up to his chest until he was in a foetal position. He decided that he would not go back to sleep, but would instead just rest his eyes and wait until he heard the others head down for breakfast. The light was now creeping past the curtains and started to lighten the room and bird song started to fill the air outside. The rain, it appeared had stopped at some point while Robert had slept, but the sheer volume had ensured that conditions outside were appalling. He lay on his pillow with his thoughts which soon turned to another faux pas involving poor Harold. He must be sick of the sight of him, Robert thought to himself. It was odd that the room was not ready though, he pondered. Once Mrs Deacon arrives she won't have a very inviting welcome; after all his room was brimming with warmth and comfort. His thoughts lingered on the pleasure derived from having been positively spoilt on his arrival; how lucky he was. But his thoughts did not last much longer after that; as once again he found himself succumbing to tiredness and drifting off into a deep, contented sleep.

Slowly Robert's awareness started to reawaken and for a brief moment he tried to decide whether or not he had been asleep, until he resolved that he must have done. Despite having his eyes firmly shut, he could tell that it was daylight outside especially as he was laid facing the window. The familiar sound of bird song drifted into his consciousness and he then became aware of a light tapping followed by the sound of his bedroom door opening behind him. Before he had the chance to react he heard footsteps enter the room and felt a light pressure on the bed and something prod at his back. Alarmed, he turned and braced himself for what was before him. But to his relief he discovered that it was nothing more sinister than a beautiful cat, which purred and prodded at Robert, desperate for his attention. Stood at the foot of the bed was the familiar, reassuring presence of Harold, who was holding in his left hand what appeared to be Robert's suit, freshly cleaned, dried and pressed. In his right hand he held a pair of shoes, which Robert recognised as his own, with the notable exception of them having been expertly polished and significantly cleaner than they had been the previous night.

"Good morning, Harold" croaked Robert, before succumbing to the pressure the cat was placing him under by stroking the top of his head; the cat purred its approval.

"Good afternoon, sir" replied Harold. "I see you've met, Morris."

"Morris!" he laughed. "What sort of name is that for a cat?"

"I believe Mr Deacon named him after his car, sir. At least that's what I've been told" Harold replied.

"This is Thomas Deacon's cat?" asked Robert. "This must have been his home then? Of course, how silly of me. Why else would we have been dragged all the way up here?"

"It is indeed Mr Deacon's cat. His pride and joy by all accounts. It certainly received more affection than any of his lady friends" said Harold. "At least, that's what I'm told, sir."

"Oh really?" asked Robert, probing. "And who told you that?"

"Oh nobody, sir, please excuse me. I'm talking out of turn" Harold replied, suddenly uncomfortable at the conversation. "I have your suit here, sir. I pressed it myself this morning. I'll leave it here and take mine back off you if that's okay, sir?"

"Yours?" Robert asked, surprised.

"Yes, sir. It's the only one we had available at such short notice, obviously, sir" Harold said. "I didn't mind at all, sir. I was only too happy to help." Robert eyed Harold up and down and estimated that the man was at least four inches shorter than him. "Is everything alright, sir?"

"Yes. Yes of course, Harold. I'm just tired that's all. I think I must have dozed off. Is everyone else down at breakfast already?"

Harold struggled to avoid smirking at Robert, "I believe that they're just about to start lunch, sir."

"What?" cried Robert, leaping naked from the bed and causing Morris to scamper out of the room. Suddenly aware of his position he once again found himself covering his genitals with his hands, whilst Harold stifled a smirk, averted his eyes and began laying his clothes out on the foot of the bed. "Why on earth didn't you wake me?"

"I did knock, sir. But you were sleeping so soundly that I decided it was best not to wake you and to ensure you had sufficient rest after last night's events" Harold replied. "Besides, chef said that a breakfast would be cooked for you when you were ready. Although you may want to just have lunch now, sir? The choice is yours."

"I best just get myself washed and dressed and downstairs. I'll eat whatever's provided thank you, Harold."

"Very good, sir" Harold replied, "I trust you remember where the bathroom is?" Robert looked at him plainly. "Of course you do, sir, apologies."

Harold left the room, shutting the door behind him. Already Robert could hear chatter downstairs and wafts of a very familiar aroma to what he had feasted on the previous night. He immediately salivated at the thought of it, but before he could eat he would have to seek out some sort of liquid refreshment. His mouth and throat were dry and sore. He opened his luggage and put fresh underwear, a clean shirt and then the freshly laundered trousers on and made his way to the bathroom.

As he opened his bedroom door, he could hear the sounds of cutlery feverishly clattering against china as well as the familiar sound of polite conversation. In addition to this there was a scratching noise much nearer to him. "Hello, Morris. What are you up to then?" Robert asked the cat. He smiled as although he was not expecting an answer the cat looked at him and meowed. He stroked under his chin, parting Morris' black fur to reveal thick cream-like fur beneath. "You're a handsome thing aren't you?" This time Morris did not respond, but continued pawing and scratching at the door. "You're an inquisitive thing aren't you?" Robert asked rhetorically, before opening the door for the cat. Robert looked in out of nosiness to see the unmade bed, just as it was the previous night, and felt the chill of a room unprepared for any occupants. Morris, meanwhile, had curled up in the corner of the room by the wardrobe, and was already asleep. "Funny thing!" Robert remarked to himself. Leaving the door ajar for the cat, he made his way to the bathroom and did his best to wash and freshen up in the limited time he felt that he had.

As he went back to the room, he glanced into the room next door and Morris was still sleeping contentedly. Robert put his clean suit jacket and perfectly polished shoes on and made his way down the stairs to the dining room, where people were still dining and the conversation was notably more fluid than it had been previously. Helped no doubt by the time the other guests had to become acquainted with each other; a fact that made Robert's stomach lurch slightly as he braced himself for walking in to a room full of strangers. He had always been one to shy away from the spotlight, so a room full of eyes turning on him at once was less than appealing.

As he descended the stairs, he noticed that all of the portraits had names at the bottom of the frame, all of which shared the surname of Deacon. Reaching the bottom he noticed that they were chronological, with Thomas Deacon's father being above the final few steps and a portrait of Thomas at the start of the hallway. As well as their names, their years of birth and death were also noted. Robert noticed that Thomas's father had died this year too; little did he know his son would soon follow him. He stood staring at the portrait of Deacon, whose eyes seemed to stare back at Robert and his face showed the recognisable sneer that he had endured all those years ago. He was older in the portrait, naturally, but it was still unmistakably Thomas Deacon; 'Thomas Deacon 1899 - …' someone needs to fill that end bit in at some stage, Robert thought to himself.

The sound of a door closing from upstairs brought Robert to his senses; he was procrastinating deliberately and it was time to join his fellow guests. As he made his way across the hallway to the dining room, the light pitter-patter of paws coming down the stairs and a chirpy meow stopped him in his tracks. Morris was purring and walking in and out of his legs in a figure of eight. Robert bent down once again, grateful to his feline friend of a timely interruption. "Hello, Morris." He cooed, stroking the cat on the top of his head. "You've got funny fur, haven't you? Is it cream or is it black. You can't make up your mind, can you?"

"And there was me thinking it was a woman's prerogative to change her mind."

Robert looked up to where the voice had come from and stood up aghast in a mixture of shock and awe. Stood at the top of the stairs, dressed in sartorial elegance and a picture of stunning beauty was none other than the famous Lilly Langham; star of the music hall, singer, dancer, actress, fantasy of every red-blooded male in the country and the woman who awakened a teenage Robert's carnal desires when he saw her at the Palladium in 1912. His father had taken him to London during the Christmas holiday; albeit that involved Robert sitting on his own in the theatre while his father waited for the show to finish just down the road from the theatre in The Argyll Arms.

As Lilly languidly sashayed down the stairs, Robert replayed that very evening in his mind while watching her perfect form gracefully descend towards him. The train journey had been a tiresome affair; full of the awkward silences you would expect from a distant father who did not know his son and who had no interest in knowing him. This was a dutiful excursion, which Robert's father could tick off before returning to the normal distance between them at their family home over the festive period. The little his father had spoken to him had mainly revolved around ensuring his studies were up to scratch, but the most interesting part was the prelude to the theatre. Robert had heard tales from the other boys at school about the famous London west end. The breeding ground for Charlie Chaplin, Stan Laurel and Fred Karno; one could expect a heady mix of slapstick, dancing girls, bawdy songs, conjurors, ventriloquism and so much more. He remembered the excitement in the queue listening to other patrons commenting on who was appearing that night; the relief when his father pointed him in the right direction with his ticket and disappeared down the road; the thrill of being dragged along in the swell of the packed crowd.

He sat in the middle of the sixth row back in the stalls and had the perfect view along with a pocketful of bon bon sweets to keep him occupied whilst waiting for the show to begin. The first half featured Paul Cinqueralli, 'King of the Jugglers', who one of his school friends said he had seen catch a cannon ball on his neck. There was no such danger on this occasion as he performed his famous human billiard table routine. Just before the interval the first half closed with Harry Champion singing his renowned 'I'm Henery the Eight, I am'; despite the audience having heard it multiple times before, they howled with laughter and cried for more. But as the curtain came down and no more was forthcoming from the Cockney comedian, the theatre emptied almost immediately as everybody rushed to the bar before the second half began. Robert stayed in his seat, of course, sucking on bon bons and looking up and around, marvelling at the high ceiling, the grand-looking boxes with their ornate golden exteriors and the bright lights above.

The second half started with a ventriloquist so bad Robert could see his lips moving. Having exhausted looking at the fineries of the theatre he turned his attention to watching the other patrons, especially a man in the row in front of him who did his best to let the ventriloquist know how bad he was. The heckling got so bad that some of the other patrons told him to 'leave the poor chap alone' and 'he can't help it if the dummy's better than he is'. As the ventriloquist left the stage, throwing filthy looks at the heckler as he went, he was replaced by the Prime minister of mirth, George Robey, to a chorus of approval from the alcohol fuelled audience. The night ended with the Queen of the Music Hall, Marie Lloyd, performing some renditions of some of her famous songs, a fitting end to a wonderful show. Somewhere in between Marie Lloyd and a female drag act was a young girl who was an unknown to the audience and did not even appear in the programme. She was introduced as Lilly Bonds and was a late addition to replace the comedic drunk act, who was rumoured amongst the audience to be ironically unresponsive in his dressing room after drinking too much whisky before the performance.

Lilly was due to be part of one of the filler acts; a group of young ladies reprising a Victorian burlesque act which had long gone out of fashion, but was at least guaranteed to keep the male interest on-going before the later headline acts. Lilly had performed in the background of that act all season, but had high aspirations and regularly petitioned the management for a spot of her own. She was clearly talented, but her tender age as well as a well-known act of indiscretion with a touring escapologist act from the United States of America had made the management circumspect. But with the comic turn incapacitated and the programme short a slot, she lobbied successfully for her opportunity and was given a one song act. The knife throwing act and a song and dance routine were then to be brought forward, allowing Lilly enough time to get changed back into her burlesque outfit to perform again with her regular act towards the end of the show.

She strode confidently out to the centre of the stage, dressed as a lady in her best fineries and holding a parasol, she was instructed to sing a song originally written for a male act, the words of which were ill-fitting for a female singer. But she delivered it with precision, grace and with comic effect and was well received with the audience. She was talented clearly, but her beauty and sex appeal were not only evident to the audience, but she was well aware of the effect that she was having on the on-looking men who cried for more. The more they brayed like donkeys, the more exaggerated her movements and confident she became.

"You are my honey, honeysuckle,

I am the bee.

I'd like to sip the honey sweet

From those red lips, you see" she sang, winking at the audience.

"I love you dearly, dearly,

And I want you to love me," she continued, posing in a risqué pose, with her rear facing the audience, looking back at them and wiggling her behind like a bumble bee, to cries of approval from the audience.

"You are my honey, honeysuckle,

I am the bee" she finished, blowing a seductive kiss and curtseying extravagantly to the audience who were in a state of hysteria and stood to applaud, cheer and beg her for more. Robert, however, remained seated; transfixed by the sight before him. He was utterly captivated and every word, every movement, and every gesture he imagined were delivered to him alone; he was oblivious to the pandemonium to his left, his right, in front and behind. She was the only thing he could see, shining brightly and beaming from centre stage.

She went to exit the stage, but stopped as she saw the manager standing in front of the knife thrower and his female assistant, waving his hand at her to indicate her to stay on. She did not need a second invitation, immediately returning to the stage and having the temerity to quieten the audience down with a finger to her pursed lips and instruct them to be re-seated by adopting a mock disapproving look on her face and pointing her finger downwards. They did as instructed immediately; submissive to her demands. Her next action was brave; some may call it reckless, but would either make or kill her career. Knowing that the headline act, Marie Lloyd, was due on later to close the show, she chose one of her most iconic songs to perform; the very song that she was due to sing last as an encore.

She leant down towards the orchestra and instructed them as to the tune she wanted, to looks of nervous alarm amongst the musicians. At first they did not comply, but after a glare at the conductor and a nod of approval from the wings by the manager, blissfully ignorant of her request, the band began to strike up the tune to 'Oh Mr Porter'. Her performance brought howls of laughter from the men in particular, along with some disapproving looks from some of the female audience. She paraded around the stage with faux-innocence, delivering the words with a knowing look to the on-looking crowd.

"Lately I just spent a week with my old Aunt Brown,
Came up to see the wondrous sights of famous London Town.
Just a week I had of it, all round the place we'd roam

Wasn't I sorry on the day I had to go back home?
Worried about with packing, I arrived late at the station,
Dropped my hatbox in the mud, the things all fell about,
Got my ticket, said 'good - bye' "Right away." the guard did cry,
But I found the train was wrong and shouted out:

Oh! Mister Porter, what shall I do?
I want to go to Birmingham
And they're taking me on to Crewe,
Send me back to London as quickly as you can,
Oh! Mister Porter, what a silly girl I am!

The porter would not stop the train, but I laughed and said 'You must
Keep your hair on, Mary Ann, and mind that you don't bust.'
Some old gentleman inside declared that it was hard,
He said 'Look out of the window, Miss, and try and call the guard.'
Didn't I, too, with all my might I nearly balanced over,
But my old friend, he grasped my leg, and pulled me back again,
Nearly fainting with the fright, I sank into his arms a sight,
Went into hysterics but I cried in vain:

Oh! Mister Porter, what shall I do?
I want to go to Birmingham
And they're taking me on to Crewe,
Send me back to London as quickly as you can,
Oh! Mister Porter, what a silly girl I am!

On his clean old shirt-front then I laid my trembling head,
"Do take it easy, rest awhile" the dear old chappie said.
If you make a fuss of me and on me do not frown,
You shall have my mansion, dear, away in London Town.
Wouldn't you think me silly if I said I could not like him?
Really he seemed a nice old boy, so I replied this way;
I will be your own for life, your I may doodle um little wife,
If you'll never tease me any more I say.

Oh! Mister Porter, what shall I do?
I want to go to Birmingham
And they're taking me on to Crewe,
Send me back to London as quickly as you can,
Oh! Mister Porter, what a silly girl I am!"

Marie Lloyd appeared on the wings, apoplectic with rage, resulting in the manager having to calm her down and only just persuaded her to take to the stage later on. Lilly carried on regardless to the adulation of the laughing, wolf-whistling crowd. Quite what was so amusing was beyond Robert at the time, but he certainly learned the true meaning of the song in hindsight. The song about the girl who went too far, delivered by a girl only four years older than Robert at the time, but one who certainly understood the meaning. She performed it to both comic and erotic effect in a way that the great Marie Lloyd, giant of the music hall, could never do. No amount of experience and talent could make up for Lloyd's lack of sexual allure; something that Lilly had naturally in abundance. After that performance she would never play burlesque again; instead appearing on a nightly basis for years to come under the name Lilly Langham, which, it was decided, was more befitting of a star. She had captured his heart completely and would be the object of his desire for years to come as well as the majority of the male population who had the fortune to see her perform. And here she stood, alone in front of him, inches away; the years that passed evidently having no negative effect on her beauty.

Robert stood, still stunned, with the tune to The Honeysuckle and the Bee fixed in his head. "Well....." she said to him, flashing him a smile. "Don't be shy. I'm Lilly" she said.

"I know who you are" was the only response he could think of. "Oh....Robert" he added. "My name's Robert."

Used to men being rendered useless in her presence, she took the lead; putting her arm around his and allowing him to lead her to the dining room. "Come on then Robert. Let's have lunch."

Chapter Eleven

"Ah, there you are Lilly. We were beginning to worry. I'm afraid we've started without you and….." he paused, waiting for clarification as to who Lilly Langham had on her arm. Robert found himself stunned into silence once again, for standing before him appeared to be none other than Thomas Deacon, the very man whose death was the cause of his being dispatched to where he now found himself. "Dear God, Lilly. Is he mute?"

"Shut up, Bernard. You may find yourself amusing but the rest of us don't" she replied. "This is Robert. Say hello to Robert everyone."

A collection of various greetings were thrown at him all at once; not that he took any of them in. He was still trying to come to terms with the sheer bizarreness of what was being played out in front of him.

"Come on Robert. There are two seats up the end. Let's sit together shall we?" she said, ushering him up the end of the dining room to be seated with their backs to the fire.

"Darnn it, Lilly. I thought you might sit next to me. Seeing as my little brother's not with us anymore, you might want to upgrade, eh?" It was at that point Robert remembered Deacon's older brother. He had never had the misfortune to meet him as he had left Baldwin's the year before Robert had started. But he had heard Thomas denigrate him in a most jealous and bitter way, based on an assumption that his parents favoured him more than Thomas. He had the same blonde hair, facial features and obnoxious way about him and Robert baulked at the thought of spending the weekend in his company.

"You should be so lucky" replied Lilly. "Excuse my brother-in-law, Robert. He has appalling manners."

"Your brother-in-law?" asked Robert, dreading her response.

"Yes, didn't you realise? I'm Thomas's widow."

"I didn't, no. I'm sorry for your loss" he lied.

"Thank you, Robert. But never mind that. He wouldn't want us all moping around for him. Let's eat shall we?" she said, sparkling in a way that belied her status of recently widowed that seemed slightly heartless to Robert.

"I must say, all of this brevity seems in dreadfully poor taste" said a voice from a woman at the other end of the table.

"Oh pack it in, Sophia. He's been dead for three months" Bernard admonished, lighting up a cigarette. This information at least explained Lilly's lack of visible grief.

"Really brother dear, some of us abhor the smell of your tobacco, and Lilly and her friend haven't even eaten yet. Why don't you take it elsewhere?" she replied.

"What and miss out on all the fun? Not on your life, Sophia. Come on then," Bernard said, turning his attention to Robert. "Who are you and where the bloody hell have you been hiding all day?"

Robert found his words stuck in his throat; it was as if he was back at school with his old nemesis once again and he had reverted back to type.

"Bloody hell!" he exclaimed. "He *is* mute" Bernard said, roaring with laughter.

"Don't be such a prick, Bernard" Lilly said, putting him back in his place. "I tell you what, why don't we all go round the table and introduce ourselves while we wait for food."

"You'll be waiting a long time then" said Bernard, "there's been no sign of anyone. We all turned up as instructed and the food was already laid out over there on the sideboard.

"Alright then," Lilly responded, "let's go and help ourselves Robert, then we'll come back and do introductions. Come on then, let's go and have a look what we've got."

"It's curry. And bloody good it is too. Not as hot as I'm used to but an excellent effort." Robert did not need to look at who had just spoken; he knew exactly who it was as surely as he knew it was the same curry he had enjoyed the previous night. Amidst the hubbub of the last few minutes, Robert had failed to actually look at each of the people sat around the table. He glanced over to his left and saw the very same man who Florence had had the altercation with in the dining cart; the same stiff manner, the same impeccably starched attire, the same emotionless soul.

"Achar gosht, if I'm not mistaken" said Robert, finding his voice.

"Bloody hell!" exclaimed Bernard, "he speaks!"

Robert noticed Lilly throw Bernard a disapproving look, while the well starched man seemed suddenly interested in Robert. "I say. That's a remarkable nose you have there, sir. You must have a great deal of experience? I had a fair deal out in India. First rate."

"At least a day's worth" Robert replied, to looks of confusion. "The chef made me the very same last night when I arrived. Other than that I've never had it before."

"Bloody favouritism!" Bernard chirped. "We got bugger all other than shown to bed by Lilly."

"Bernard will you please shut up" said Lilly, irritated. She turned and immediately radiated towards Robert, smiling "come on then. Let's try some!"

She oozed confidence and charm and seemed to have the whole room in the palm of her hand; she certainly had a firm hold over the elder Deacon sibling. Despite the sheer horror of hearing that Thomas Deacon had somehow managed to meet and marry her, Robert could not help but be utterly captivated by her, once again.

Her star had long since waned and younger people may not have even heard of her; but people of a certain age were more than aware of who Lilly Langham was. Having established herself as a bona fide star of the music hall, she had followed the path of many a British star of the stage and travelled to Hollywood. The Stepney Songbird, as the press had dubbed her, arrived in Hollywood in a blaze of glory in 1918 after six years at the top in London. She had monopolised the nation's hearts; commanded the highest fees; and had a string of high profile men all clamouring to be seen with her in the nation's capital. Hollywood was the natural progression for her; a bigger stage and a much bigger audience.

The First World War had ended but its impact on films would last forever. America was the only major nation to survive the war with its economy in a similar position to when it had entered the conflict. The French, German and Russian film industries all contracted in the aftermath, allowing the American industry to flower. As it expanded it sought new stars to fill its screens. Negotiations began in 1917 with the Mutual Film Company to bring Lilly over to Hollywood to star as Charlie Chaplin's leading lady. By the time Lilly had agreed her contract and then finalised her contractual obligations in England, our greatest export to Hollywood, Charlie Chaplin, had just left Mutual to form his own production company, First National. There was an attempt by Lilly to join Chaplin at First National, but he had no interest in starring with her; preferring to continue with his established partner, Edna Purviance. By New Year's Eve of that very year, the Mutual Film Company ceased to exist and Lilly, despite having been paid handsomely, had made precisely no appearances on the silver screen.

Unknown in the United States, she struggled to command the same demand she had in England. Some forgettable minor cameo parts followed in various slapstick films starring minor comedians of the time, until in 1921 she got her big break. She successfully auditioned for the part of the leading lady opposite Roscoe Fatty Arbuckle in a feature film, entitled 'The Cincinnati Scoundrel'. Arbuckle invited Lilly over to meet him at a hotel in San Fransisco, where he was partying with friends. Lilly had arrived amidst hedonistic drunken scenes that were not uncommon in Hollywood and sought Arbuckle out to introduce herself to him. Arbuckle took time out to meet her and she stayed for a few drinks, to ingratiate herself with her new co-star. Lilly behaved herself, resisted the amorous attentions of several men, including Arbuckle and left the party once Roscoe had moved his attentions elsewhere. Two days later, Virginia Rappe, a guest at the party, was hospitalised due to injuries her friend claimed were received at the party at Arbuckle's hand. A day later she was dead. Arbuckle was arrested, tried for her murder, and then subsequently exonerated after his accuser was proved to be a fraud. The damage to Hollywood, and more specifically Arbuckle's reputation was significant. From 1920 Hollywood had been plagued in scandal; actress Olive Thomas's death by accidental poisoning after she drank her husband's syphilis topical medication; the murder of William Desmond Taylor, which ruined the career of Arbuckle's long time screen partner, Mabel Normand; Wallace Reid's drug related death; and Thomas Ince's mysterious death aboard William Randolph Hearst's yacht. The Film Industry sought to distance themselves from those involved so as not to tarnish themselves; as a result Arbuckle's films were banned and he was ostracized by all but those who knew him best. The same fate fell on all those at the party, assumed guilty by their association. 'The Cincinnati Scoundrel' was never made and Lilly Langham's Hollywood career was over.

After the scandal she disappeared from the public view after several attempts to resurrect her career had failed. Her stock in America was non-existent, whilst she had long since been replaced in the nation's heart back in England and so she disappeared from the public eye. Robert had thought of her on occasions and often wondered where she had ended up; and now he knew. She had married Thomas Deacon and was residing in a remote area on the West Coast of Scotland.

Now the only role she played was that of dutiful host, and was playing it with aplomb. She lifted up the silver lid of the first chaffing dish to reveal a mound of rice, "let me be mother" said Lilly, smiling broadly at Robert again. She seemed to be taking him under her wing, perhaps sensing his initial trepidation. She spooned two portions of the fluffy rice onto the plates that Robert was holding, steam wafting from it after it had been kept warm from the candles underneath the dish. She then unveiled the curry which looked exactly the same as it had the night before. Lilly smelt the wafts of pungent air from the dish as it rose and made a delightful contented sound, "Oooh that smells delightful. I hope it tastes as good as it looks."

She began to spoon out the delicious looking curry onto the plates; Robert swallowed hard as the smell hit his senses. "I'm surprised your chef has never cooked it for you before?" Robert asked, picking up on her comment.

"My chef? Oh I see" she replied, "Oh no. I don't live here in this God forsaken place. This is one of many little bolt holes

Thomas had tucked away. We brought the chef and Harold in just for this weekend. They arrived yesterday not long after we all did."

"We?" replied Robert. "I assumed you were here already?"

"Oh no." said Lilly, putting some bread on the plates, "I came up on the train with everybody else. I saw you in the dining cart in fact, you were obviously too preoccupied at the time! Shall we?"

"Shall we…?" the words lingered in the air.

"Sit down and eat, Robert?" she replied, patiently.

"Oh yes of course." He cursed himself for being so distracted, although he was not surprised given the circumstances.

"Come on you two. We haven't got all day you know" said Bernard, impatiently.

"Oh really?" replied Lilly, patronising him, "have you got anything more pressing planned? A nice walk, perhaps? Or maybe a spot of fishing?"

"Ha!" He snorted. "Not bloody likely in this weather. Have you seen it out there? It's blowing up a bloody treat."

Everyone looked to the windows and it had got distinctly darker over-head. The trees were creaking and straining against the wind which looked for all intents and purposes like it was hell bent on destruction. Rain began to hit the window as suddenly as it had appeared in Glasgow the previous day.

"It's awful isn't it?" said Lilly. "Still this curry's nice and warm. Blimey! It's really warm in fact." She said, coughing.

"Here, my dear" the stuffed shirt said, and poured her a glass of red wine, finishing the bottle in the process. Robert smirked to himself at the reminder of his exchange with Florence, but then immediately regretted it as he thought of her subsequent violent death.

"Thank you, Mr Brannigan" said Lilly, smiling at him. "Aren't you sweet?"

"Oh, call me Charles." He blushed slightly and looked decidedly hot under the collar. If anyone could extract an emotion from him, how obvious that it would be Lilly, thought Robert.

"Come on then" Lilly insisted. "Let's go round the table. Robert I'm Lilly and…."

"Oh for God's sake, Lilly!" interrupted Bernard. "The whole bloody world knows who you are."

"Not anymore they don't" came a hushed barb from the other female, to which Lilly threw her a distinctly cold stare.

"Now then, sister dear, there was no need for that!" Bernard said, although it seemed to amuse him somewhat.

Lilly returned to her role of facilitator, turning her look of disapproval to one of radiant hostess once again. "Robert, do you indeed know who I am?"

Bernard rolled his eyes. "For heaven's sake, get on with it."

Lilly had not stopped looking and smiling at Robert while she waited for his response. "I know exactly who you are" Robert assured her, in a soothing and measured tone which implied everything he wanted it to. Yes he knew her, yes she was beautiful, and yes he adored her.

She smiled knowingly at him, her blue eyes sparkling. "Thank you Robert. Now let's continue shall we?" she said looking at Robert. Silence ensued before he realised other than his first name, nobody knew him either.

"I'm Robert Johnson." A glance down the table confirmed that there were seven pairs of eyes trained on him. His audience sat there, waiting for more. Awkward at the silence, Robert continued as briefly as he could muster to divert the attention on to someone else. "There's not much to say really. I work in London, I'm widowed," at which the other female hung more intently on his words, "that's it really."

Unsatisfied with his meager response they began to question him. "So were you a pal of Thomas's then?" asked Bernard.

"Not at all" replied Robert, "no offence to you but far from it. We roomed at school, but other than that…."

"Oh so you'd know Max then?" asked Bernard.

"Max?" enquired Robert.

"I'm afraid we've not had the pleasure" said the man next to Bernard. "Yet" he added. "No I replaced Robert once he......left Baldwin's" he said, smirking.

"Oh bloody hell, of course. You're the one who nearly killed Thomas playing cricket. Ha!" snorted Bernard, "no wonder you two didn't get on then" he laughed. "Well what the hell are you doing here then? Bit late to finish the job off, old boy. Somebody got in there first!"

"Please don't say that" said the female. "You know that Lilly said that it was an accident."

"Of course it was, Sophia, of course it was" mocked Bernard. "Well Robert. I'm Bernard; Thomas's better looking older brother. Pleased to meet you. No hard feelings on my part. He always was a little shit."

"Bernard, please" exclaimed the female, "you mustn't speak ill of the dead."

"Let's move on shall we?" said Lilly. "Thank you, Bernard, helpful as usual. Max, you're next."

Sat next to Bernard Deacon was the man who clearly knew about the ignominious departure of Robert from school. He had greasy looking black hair, slicked back revealing a widow's peak, which made his thin, pointed face look even more rook-like. "Max Kinkaid, Robert. Charmed to meet you" he said. "I have had the pleasure of sleeping in your bed."

Robert's brow furrowed and eyes looked alarmed. "I beg your pardon?"

"Hang on, old chap!" spluttered Bernard, "I didn't have you pinned for that sort of thing, Robert?"

Max smirked and the female next to him looked pained at the proceedings. "Like I said" added Max, "I haven't had the pleasure. Yet."

"MAX!" exclaimed Lilly, disapprovingly.

Max sucked at the end of his cigarette and blew smoke in Robert's direction and looked at him intently with his piercing brown eyes, eyeing him up and down. It made Robert's skin crawl.

"Kindly explain yourself" said Robert, putting his knife and fork down on his plate. Lilly put her hand on his to calm him, which stopped him in his tracks for a moment. The feel of her soft skin on his was a surreal experience amidst the juxtaposition of the repulsion he had felt seconds earlier.

Max blew more smoke from his mouth. "I started Baldwin's the day after you were kicked out. Naturally they gave me your bed as it had recently been vacated. I'm not convinced they'd even changed the sheets. I could smell someone's scent on the pillows."

Lilly squeezed his hand tightly. "Pack it in, Max. You're not his type" Bernard quipped, smacking him playfully on the arm.

Max slouched back in his chair and continued to smoke, not taking his eyes off Robert for a moment. Lilly's hand remained on Robert's for the duration of the introductions, to his pleasure.

"Sophia. Your turn" said Lilly.

The woman next to Max, who continued to suck hard on his cigarette and expel wafts of smoke across the table, smiled at Robert genuinely. Thus far she had appeared irritated by some of the comments but appeared to draw a line under her previous emotions. "Hello Robert, I'm Sophia Kinkaid, Max's wife and Thomas and Bernard's little sister. I'm very pleased to meet you."

"I'm pleased to meet you too, Sophia. I'm sorry for your loss" replied Robert, sensing that she at least seemed genuinely remorseful at her brother's death. She also, bore no resemblance to her brothers in terms of their brash arrogance and sense of entitlement. The only similarities in fact were her undeniable good looks, blue eyes and blonde hair, which she wore down, long and natural-looking. She seemed sensitive and genuine; the very antithesis of what he would have expected, and given whom she was married to, Robert saw her in a positive light.

"Thank you, Robert. How very sweet of you to say that" she replied.

"That's better" said Lilly, approving of the more civil exchanges. "Alistair, it's your turn now."

"Hello Robert, I'm Alistair Rashford" boomed the man to Sophia's left who had thus far remained silent. He stood and strode confidently over to Robert and shook him firmly by the hand. "Don't mind those bloody fools over there. We'll have a chat later sensibly, eh? Without Laurel and Hardy over there," he said nodding his head towards Max and Bernard, "and their double act."

"Hey," said Bernard, "which one am I supposed to be?" Max remained silent, but stubbed his cigarette out on his plate.

"Max really. Is there any need for that?" Sophia asked, to which Robert noticed that he looked at her with disdain.

"I was Thomas's business partner" continued Alistair. "We were working on a project up here in Scotland. Well, I say we, I actually. Thomas had been overseas for some time and the lures of Knoydart weren't strong enough to attract him from California. His loss though eh?!" he quipped, slapping Robert on the back.

"Talking of sunny Knoydart, why the bloody hell did you drag us up here, Lilly? This could have been done in England couldn't it?" Bernard complained, looking out of the window at the incessant rain beating against the windows.

"I've told you already," said Lilly, "blame your brother. It was part of the terms of the will to have it read here. There's nothing you or I could do about it, even if we wanted to. So 'sunny Knoydart' it is!"

"Interesting word, Knoydart" said a voice, previously unheard by Robert, which prompted Bernard to sigh with impatience. "Loosely translated it means both loch heaven as well as loch hell."

"Well which one is it? It can't be both, surely?" asked Lilly.

"I suppose that depends on why you've come here" said Max in between puffs of his cigarette, his words the prelude to a brief moment of silence until it was punctured by the effervescence of Lilly.

"That's very interesting, Dr Hawthorne. Robert, this is Dr Hawthorne." Lilly said, taking over proceedings after the doctor had resumed his thoughtfulness.

"I'm Pleased to meet you, Doctor Hawthorne" said Robert. The doctor merely smiled and nodded in Robert's direction.

"And last but not least, we have the lovely Charles" said Lilly, introducing the final guest.

"Charles Brannigan" he said, stretching out his hand towards Robert for him to shake. "I'm pleased to meet you, Robert. Although of course we've already met, albeit not on a named basis."

"Really?" said Bernard, leaning forward over the table towards Robert. "Do tell, old chap. Brannigan here has not been very liberal with an explanation as to why he's here." The door opened and Harold walked in to begin clearing lunch away but everybody was too engrossed in the conversation to notice.

"I've no idea, I'm afraid. We merely shared a train carriage…briefly. Well?" asked Robert. "Why are you here, Mr Brannigan?"

Brannigan finished his wine and put his empty glass down on the table. "Because I hoped someone might kill me."

Sophia gasped in horror, "Surely you don't mean that, Mr Brannigan?"

"Of course he doesn't, Sophia" scolded Max.

"You're a rum fellow" laughed Bernard. "Fancy coming out with that!"

Robert did not find the comment amusing, and did not believe that was its intention either. Having witnessed the exchange on the train, he found the comment deeply disturbing. Harold picked up another bottle of red wine from the sideboard, opened it and returned to the table; standing over Brannigan he held the bottle over his empty glass. "More wine, Captain?"

Brannigan looked up at Harold, who remained at the ready with the red wine and looking directly into Brannigans eyes. It was at this point Robert noticed that Harold had a scar on his face that was not present yesterday. "No, thank you" replied Brannigan, "I believe I've had enough." He stood and placed his serviette over his empty plate. "Would you excuse me, my dear Miss Langham? It's been a pleasure." He took Lilly's hand and kissed it gently, then calmly left the room, closing the door behind him.

"What on earth was all that about. Isn't he a queer fellow?" quipped Bernard, who was, however, the only person in the room who appeared undisturbed by Brannigan's departure. A departure not too dissimilar to the one Robert had witnessed the day before on the train; and that had been the prelude to murder.

"I'm dreadfully sorry, Miss Langham" said Harold, "I thought you'd all have finished lunch by now. I'll come back later once Mr Johnson and you have finished; after I've poured the wine, of course." He filled Robert's glass.

"Thank you, Harold. That will be all for now" said Lilly, who picked up her cutlery and began eating her lunch again. Robert looked down at his own plate which had barely been touched; he had suddenly lost his appetite. Around the table the remaining guests began speculating on the nature of Brannigan's comment, other than the doctor, who sat smiling at nothing in particular and Lilly who ate with visible delight with every mouthful."

Robert went to pick up the glass but Lilly swung her hand out to hold his, asking "So Robert, tell me. What do you do for fun?" and knocking his drink all over his lap. "Oh Robert," she gasped in horror. "What have I done?"

Robert looked down at himself and saw his freshly laundered suit splattered in red wine, and his white shirt ruined. Harold glared at Lilly, "I'll fetch Mr Johnson a change of clothes again, Miss Langham."

"Never mind that," interrupted Bernard, "don't hog that wine, there's a good chap." As Lilly fussed over Robert, dabbing him with a serviette, Bernard took the wine bottle and went round the table, receiving declines from both of the ladies, the doctor and Alistair. "Just you and me then Max, old chap" he said, filling up Max's glass. As Bernard returned to the table and sat down to pour himself a drink, the polite conversation was brought to a shattering end as the sound of a gunshot echoed throughout the house.

Sophia screamed in shock, Bernard dropped the wine bottle which smashed onto the wooden floor, while the others paused momentarily in silence, processing what they had heard before they ran towards where the sound had come from. Alistair and Robert were first upstairs and headed by direction from Lilly at the rear towards the bedroom that belonged to Brannigan. As they burst into the room, the scene before them was clear cut; Charles Brannigan had taken his own life. The revolver was still in his hand and there was a single gunshot to his temple.

Chapter Twelve

Dr Hawthorne examined the body as the other guests looked on with a mixture of horror, pity and bewilderment. Harold arrived at the door just as the shock of the situation hit Sophia, who made a low shrill noise and fell against Robert's chest.

"Good catch, old chap. Perhaps you weren't so bad at cricket after all!" Bernard quipped to a look of disapproval from Robert.

"Hardly the time for cracking jokes is it?" Robert replied.

"Quite right, poor taste indeed." added Alistair. "Here, let me give you a hand. Lilly, which room is she in? Let's lay her down on her bed."

"It's fine" said Robert, "I can manage." Sophia was tall for a woman, but slender in build. Robert scooped her up in his arms and following Lilly, carried her to her room, leaving the remaining guests with Brannigan's corpse.

"Shouldn't her husband be doing this?" asked Robert.

"What Max?" Lilly replied, scoffing. "He's not really the chivalrous type, in case you hadn't noticed."

"I had. How did she end up with such a creep? The man is positively repulsive" Robert added, as he laid Sophia down on one of two single beds.

"You'll get no disagreement from me on that. Poor Sophia! From what I understand her father arranged the marriage with the Kinkaids. No doubt there was some sort of financial incentive for him in such an alliance. Bernard didn't do anything for anyone unless there was something in it for him."

"Bernard?" asked Robert, confused.

"Yes, the Bernard that you've had the misfortune of meeting was named after his father. Daddy's blue eyed boy; literally. It was a great source of bitterness for Thomas, I can assure you. Nothing he could do was ever right. He wasn't as academic as his brother; he wasn't as sporty as his brother; the part of the family business that Thomas was entrusted with didn't make as much money as Bernard's. Ha!" she laughed.

"What?" asked Robert

"Poor Thomas. He even married the great Lilly Langham, to show his father what a man he was. And all he did was remind him of what happened at school."

"What do you mean? What happened?"

"Never mind, it's ancient history now. But let's just say that you're not the only man who Max had a fancy for."

Sophia groaned from her bed as she started to rouse. "I'll fetch the doctor" said Robert, and promptly made his way back to Brannigan's room while Lilly stayed with Sophia. As Robert walked along the hallway he was met by everybody else walking in the other direction, led by Harold and Alistair who between them were carrying Brannigan's lifeless corpse.

"What's going on?" asked Robert.

"Dr Hawthorne suggested we keep Mr Brannigan in the coldest part of the house, for obvious reasons" answered Bernard. "The old chap might start to kick up a bit of a stink otherwise."

Upon hearing the commotion, Lilly had made her way to find out what was happening. "Bernard!" she exclaimed. "Really, can you show a bit more respect? Where are you taking her, Harold?"

"We're putting him in Mrs Deacon's room, Miss Langham. It'll be the coldest room" replied Harold, who was making his way into the room backwards with his arms under Brannigan's armpits. Alistair followed, holding the bottom of each of his thighs and they placed him face up on the nearside of the double bed. Alistair pulled his eyelids down and placed a blanket over him for dignity's sake.

"What a shame" said Alistair, solemnly as he stood next to the body. "I wonder what drove him to do it?"

"I say, Harold, you referred to him as Captain, downstairs" said Bernard, "what was that about exactly? Do you know something we don't?"

Before Harold could answer, the normally taciturn Dr Hawthorne interjected. "Charles Brannigan was an officer in his Majesty's army, as well as serving Queen Victoria in India, I believe. It was from his service in the Great War that I knew him, however, where I served in a medical capacity, naturally. I believe this explains the comment at the dinner table" he said, looking at Harold. "Does it not, Private Smith?"

All eyes focused on Harold whose grave expression did not change. "That is correct, doctor. I served under him in France, as you are well aware. If that is all, Miss Langham, I'll be going downstairs to check whether chef needs any help preparing dinner."

"Somebody needs to send word to the Police, surely. We can't do nothing about our friend here" Bernard interjected. "It's not right having a corpse hanging about the place. And at any rate, when is this bloody will being read so we can all get back to normality?"

"Mr Worthington has been unable to get here yet due to the weather" replied Harold. "He was due over this morning but it's not safe to travel by boat until this storm settles down. And I'm afraid no one will be able to send word to the Police either. Without the boats running we have the same problem getting to the mainland. The only choice would be to walk but that carries its own dangers in this weather."

"I'm afraid Harold's right" Lilly confirmed. "We'll have to just sit tight and wait for the storm to pass." This news was met with looks of concern and minor rumblings as people glanced at each other, uncomfortable with the current position they faced. "Don't worry everyone. We have a well-stocked drinks cabinet and chef has something special lined up for tonight. Come on, why don't we all have a drink. See the Captain off in style, eh?"

"Well I guess there's nothing else to do" said Bernard. "It beats hanging around here in the freezing cold with a stiff. Why is it so cold in here anyway? And when exactly is our beloved step mother gracing us with her presence?"

"I believe Mrs Deacon has been delayed" said Harold.

"Good" replied Bernard. "Bloody leach. I dare say she'll be happy to take what's coming to her from the will though."

"Come on everyone. Let's not discuss this over the Captain as he lay there. It doesn't seem right" added Lilly, leading everyone from the room, down the stairs and back into the dining room. They all entered to be greeted by Max who had remained unmoved by the goings on upstairs and was still sat in his seat smoking and drinking red wine.

"I helped myself to another bottle, Lilly. Hope you don't mind" he said. "Some clot dropped the last one."

Harold was already on his hands and knees picking up the remnants of the glass bottle and wiping the spilt wine up with some serviettes from the table. "Help yourself Max, but you might want to go and check on poor Sophia; she's had a nasty shock. Poor Captain Brannigan has…."

"Shot himself?" Max added. "You don't say. I can't understand why you all had to run up there after him. And as for you, Bernard, that was a 1912 vintage. Damn waste."

"Really Max, I'm serious" Lilly replied. "Sophia was in quite a state. Robert had to lay her on her bed to recover."

"I bet he did. Don't get any ideas, old boy. She's a married woman" he replied, smirking and then placing his cigarette back in his mouth, revisited his habit of blowing smoke provocatively towards Robert. Lilly, sensing how much he was getting under Robert's skin, swiftly took him by the arm towards the sideboard.

"Come on Robert, you can lend a hand getting everyone a drink. What'll it be everyone?" Lilly said, trying her best to carry on regardless as any host worth her salt would do. Robert, however, found it less easy to simply plough ahead with conviviality whilst there was a dead body upstairs in Mrs Deacon's room. He helped Lilly pour drinks whilst Harold remained indisposed, removing dripping serviettes from the room and clearing the table.

"Let's take these to the billiard room, shall we" suggested Lilly. "Harold will want to prepare the room for dinner tonight and perhaps a spot of billiards will serve as a welcome distraction?"

"If you say so" replied Max. "I'm quite comfortable here though." He rose from his chair and staggered slightly, grabbing hold of the table to steady his balance.

"I say old chap, you want to take more water with it" mocked Bernard.

"Piss off!" replied Max, picking up his glass and draining it in one. He refilled it and made his way to the Billiard room, past Bernard, throwing him a look of disdain as he did so.

"Only teasing, Max, only teasing" Bernard uttered with a smile. "You can get your own back on the Billiard table. I say, let's make a game of it shall we. Robert can take on Alistair and the winners play in the final."

"That's the spirit, Bernard" said Lilly, pleased that some light distraction was being offered. "But what about Dr Hawthorne, who's he going to play?"

"Well he's not here" said Max. "He must be upstairs playing with himself." Robert looked at him with disgust; he was a most repulsive man and seemed to delight in showing it.

"Here we go" said Lilly, pulling a dust sheet off the table. "You boys start will you, and I'll put some music on." Lilly made her way to the corner of the room and put a record on the gramophone, whilst the other guests congregated around the billiard table. Robert took a seat away from the others; there had been far too much death around him for his liking. He looked around the room which had oak panelling from floor to waist height and then striped blue and white wallpaper to the ceiling. Landscape pictures adorned the walls and the ceiling had ornate plaster work and coving with a chandelier offering excellent lighting on the green baize below.

The billiards game was offering much amusement to all and Robert gleaned from comments that Max was being soundly beaten by Bernard. Robert was pleased by this, although he stopped short of actually rooting for Bernard; he merely disliked him less than he did Max. He looked over to the far corner of the room to Lilly, who was dancing with herself; not for the benefit of others, but almost because her feet seemed under a spell from the music. Robert was unsure of the tune but she was performing some sort of Charleston-style swivel dance just with her feet, whilst her hands cradled a gin and tonic. She was in a world of her own and quite oblivious to Robert gazing at her. What a natural performer she was, Robert thought to himself, even when she did not intend to be.

Lilly then made eye contact with Robert and immediately laughed as she realized that he had been watching her impromptu performance. "People used to pay good money to see that, you know" she said, raising her voice above the sound of the music and then continued dancing but towards Robert.

"I know," he replied. "I was one of them!"

"Really? That must have been a long time ago, I'd left the country when I was twenty three" said Lilly, sidling up to where Robert was sat. He perched nearer the edge of the seat to continue the conversation.

"I was thirteen. You weren't called Lilly Langham then though. Not until the following night in fact."

"Blimey! You were there that night were you? I caused quite a storm that evening, I can tell you. I thought Marie Lloyd was going to smack me one, or bite me with those bloody great teeth of hers."

Robert smiled and looked downwards; he was never one for small talk and here he was faced with the formidable confidence of Lilly Langham. "So what do you do for fun, Robert?" said Lilly, trying to coax him out of his shell.

"Fun? I've forgotten what that is" he replied.

"Nonsense!" Lilly exclaimed, grabbing his hand. "Come on, up you get! Let's have a dance."

"Oh God, no! I don't dance" Robert said with sheer panic in his eyes.

"Rubbish! Come on....oh bugger!" she cursed. The record had finished and the only sound to be heard was billiard balls clanking into each other, followed by raucous noise from the onlookers. "Wait there, I'll just put another record on."

Robert saw his opportunity and seized it; as much as he would dance all night with her in his head, in reality his two left feet and lack of self-confidence meant that an escape to refill his glass in the dining room was a much more attractive option.

"Hey where are you off to?" she cried.

"I'll be back, don't worry" he replied, tapping his empty glass with his finger. "Just getting another drink."

"But there's a bar in here…..Robert?" she called; but it was too late. The sound of the music drowned her words and he had left the room. As he crossed the hallway towards the dining room, the lively tune kicked up a pace in the billiard room as well as further cheers from the game. He poured himself another glass of wine, took a deep breath and then left to return to the frivolous party which had quickly evolved after the earlier tragedy.

He was just in front of the billiard room door when he heard footsteps from the stairs; turning to see who it was his breath was taken away at the sight in front of him. Sophia made her way towards him and he stopped to wait for her. As she walked he was struck by how wonderful she looked; gone was the demure attire she had been wearing earlier as well as the behaviour that suggested she was routinely subjugated by Max and Bernard. She now carried with her an air of confidence and purpose, displayed as she glided over towards him, carrying a brandy glass in one hand with her other hand down by her side. She wore an ornate, floor-length white maxi dress with delicate raised white patterning and see-through mesh on her shoulders; the material looked soft and delicate. Her shoulders were exposed through the mesh and the neckline was v necked, partially exposing her chest; not in an overtly provocative way, but in a subtle manner. The top half of the dress was snug and perfectly fitted, accentuating her shapely figure, and had a triangle shaped cut out detail to the back of the bodice exposing her skin. As it reached her slender waist it became looser, giving way to a long, flowing and graceful floor-length skirt.

"I wonder if you wouldn't mind filling my glass, Mr Johnson. Dr Hawthorne prescribed me brandy to help with the shock."

"Of course" replied Robert, smiling. "Come with me."

She linked her arm around his and approached the dining room; evoking memories of earlier when Lilly had done the same. Lilly had very much done the leading then; almost pulling Robert towards the dining room. Sophia, on the other hand, whilst prompting the action, was happy for Robert to take the lead.

"Ladies first" he said, opening the door for her. She smiled, demurely and showing just a glimpse of her teeth beneath her delicate lips, and then entered the room with Robert following her.

He took her glass and filled it to just under halfway. "Don't tease; you can fit more than that in there. If you're going to do it for me, then do it right" she said playfully.

"Are you sure you can take it?" asked Robert. "You've had quite a shock. I wouldn't want you being ill later. Either that or have some water with it?"

"Screw your water" she said, taking the glass from him. "I didn't have you down for someone of half measures, Robert."

"I'm not sure what you mean?" he replied.

"I want you to give it to me. Not half of it, all of it" she said, leaning into him.

"Fine" he replied smiling, "I'll put more brandy in for you."

"I'm not talking about the fucking brandy" she said purposefully, placing the glass on the sideboard. Her words seemed out of character and shocked Robert. She was now an inch from him and he could feel her breath on his face, whilst her eyes bore into his, shining a vibrant, bright blue. She bit her lip seductively and her eyelashes fluttered at him. "Tell me, Robert. Could you ever love a Deacon?"

"I'm not sure that's appropriate, is it?" he replied.

"I don't want you to be appropriate. I want you to fuck me."

Robert swallowed and was unsure what to say to her. "Well" she purred softly. "Are you going to fuck me or not?" She put her right thigh against his and then whilst leaning against him, rotated around until her bottom was pressed against his groin. She stared back at him over her shoulder and fluttered her eyelashes again, whilst gently rubbing her bottom against him and leaning her cheek against his face. Robert started to become aroused and it took every ounce of self-control that he had not to kiss her passionately and take her right there over the table. As he became more aroused against her she sighed with pleasure and rubbed herself against him more. He could see that the skin on her back and chest was unblemished and smooth like alabaster. He could smell a scent on her akin to some sort of fruit; it was intoxicating and she smelt almost edible.

He weakened and kissed her neck, wrapping his arms around her stomach and pulling her against him; at which point she pulled herself away from him and approached the table. She placed the palms of her hands against the table and bent over, then turned her head to face him. "Well? What are you waiting for?"

"I can't" he replied, shaking his head.

Sophia gasped in horror. "You can't? What the hell do you mean you can't? It didn't feel like you had any objections when you were pressing yourself against me."

"It's not right" he insisted. "What about Max?"

"Max! What's he got to do with it? You don't want to fuck him do you?" she blasted, incredulous with rage.

"Of course I don't want to fuck Max."

"Well I'd watch your drink then" she replied, approaching him again.

"What do you mean?"

"If you don't want Max to fuck you then keep an eye on your drink. Let's just say he has a terrible habit of getting what he wants, whether the other person wants it or not."

"What!" he exclaimed. "You mean he uses force?"

"He doesn't need to. He just makes sure the other person has something suitable in their drink. Talking of which…." she picked up her glass and drank it down in one.

"How do you know this?" asked Robert.

"Because I know someone he did it to on more than one occasion" she replied, to Robert's disbelief. "Oh yes. Dear Max loves to fuck a Deacon, just not this one. He'll be on the lookout for someone else now poor Thomas is dead. So my advice to you is to watch out.

So are you still worried about hurting poor Max's feelings now?"

"Who's hurting my feelings?" They both looked towards the door and Max had entered, looking more than slightly the worse for wear. "What's going on here?" he snapped, accidentally spitting down his chin in the process.

"Nothing Max" Sophia replied, "Robert was just getting me a drink."

"Bullshit!" he barked, spitting again. "There's a perfectly good bar in the billiard room."

"Well what are you doing in here then?" asked Sophia, sarcastically.

"I'd come to find Robert. We can't start the next game without him. I didn't expect him to be in here with my wife though!"

"Wife, ha!" she scoffed. "The dutiful little wife for my strong, loving husband. Ha! I thought I'd find myself a real man for a change. Seems I was barking up the wrong tree there too,"

"Oh really" said Max, who approached Robert with an unpleasant leer. "How interesting. Not a fan of the fairer sex then?" He was uncomfortably close and Robert had an unpleasant sense of déjà vu. This time, however, all he could smell was alcohol and tobacco being breathed on him and Max's skin was sallow and he was sweating profusely from his forehead.

"Leave him alone!" screamed Sophia, the years of hurt and torment of her marriage unleashed at once. Her response had stopped Max in his tracks and he turned to face her, sneering. "What's wrong, Sophia. Couldn't he get it up for you either?" She slapped him full on the side of the face with the back of her hand and he fell against the sideboard, knocking her brandy glass to the floor and shattering it.

Lilly appeared at the door with a look of grave concern, having been alerted by Sophia's scream. "Whatever's the matter? What's happened?" she asked.

"My wife appears to have lost her mind" Max replied, wiping a small speck of blood from his lips where she had caught him with her ring. "I'll leave you and lover boy to finish whatever you were up to" he hissed as he staggered from the room, leaving Sophia in tears and Lilly with a look of disappointment towards Robert.

"Come on Sophia, let's get you tidied up" Lilly said, putting her arm around her. "It appears you are making quite the stir, Robert" she added, leaving with Sophia.

Robert sighed and finished his wine. Looking down at his shirt that was stained red from the wine Lilly had spilt down him and then the smashed brandy glass, it evoked images of the train carriage which held Florence's body. Leaning against the sideboard he closed his eyes and tried to make sense of it all; Florence's murder; her poor maid who looked so fragile and helpless stood covered in blood from the jugular she had pierced in the toilet; Brannigan's suicide; the whole dysfunctional farce that was the Deacon family. So much death seemed far too coincidental but Robert's mind was too addled with alcohol and tiredness to make sense of it all. He exhaled audibly in frustration, then refilled his glass and made his way back to the Billiard Room.

Chapter Thirteen

With Lilly upstairs consoling Sophia, the music had ceased in the Billiard Room and the loss of her exuberance had led to a more sedate atmosphere. In Robert's absence, Dr Hawthorne had returned and was playing Alistair at billiards, Bernard was leant against the bar watching the game unfold, whilst Max was slumped in a chair asleep.

"Robert old chap, come over here and tell me all about it" slurred Bernard from across the room. "I hear you've been dallying with my little sister. You rogue you" he mocked. Robert ignored him and hovered over the billiard table watching Dr Hawthorne convincingly outplay his opponent.

"You're a man of many talents, doctor" said Alistair, to which the doctor merely smiled knowingly and continued to play. Up close Dr Hawthorne looked younger than Robert had first thought, his years perhaps inflated in Robert's mind due to the predominant grey hair in his beard and moustache.

Unhappy at having been ignored, Bernard approached Robert to continue to bait him. "I say old chap, don't be a spoilsport. Sophia's a pretty little thing, I don't blame you. Dashed poor form though, what with her husband being in the next room and unable to defend her honour, eh" he said, nudging Robert in the ribs.

"I can assure you I did nothing inappropriate" replied Robert in a low voice designed to be as discreet as possible.

"There's no point trying to hide it old boy. Max came in and told us the whole sordid story. Caught red-handed, eh? There's no denying it, old boy."

"Whatever he said is untrue, he has no idea what happened" replied Robert, who was now quite irritated at the exchange.

"Oh so something *did* happen then" laughed Bernard. "I knew I'd catch you out in the end."

"Bernard, leave Robert alone. You can be such an insufferable bore at times" said Lilly, sweeping into the room. "Sophia's feeling better but is having a lie down."

"Well there you go, Robert, there's a fine invitation for you. Go and finish the job off, eh" said Bernard, nudging Robert in the ribs again and sloshing red wine all over his shoes in the process. "Hey Lilly!" he slurred, "Let's get the music back on and have a dance, me and you, eh. What do you say?"

"No I think I'll go and have a lie down myself. Perhaps it will do me good to get some beauty sleep and then feel refreshed for dinner."

"That's the ticket, old girl. Thought you'd never ask" said Bernard, who grew more inebriated by the minute. He grabbed at her behind and received a slap in the face from Lilly for his trouble.

"I think you've had enough drink Bernard, perhaps you should have some sleep yourself?" Lilly shot him an icy stare and swept out of the room, only to be followed by Bernard who continued to unsuccessfully cajole her. Eventually the sound of them bickering had faded and the only thing to be heard was the heavy rain beating down against the windows and Max's incessant snoring.

"Well, I think I'll follow Lilly's advice and have a lie down myself" said the doctor. "All this excitement is not good for one's blood pressure. Gentleman" he nodded to both Alistair and Robert and left the room.

"Well" said Alistair. "Just the two of us left, Robert. Fancy a game?"

"I don't play, I'm afraid" said Robert.

"Let's sit and have a drink then. Come on, what's your poison?" said Alistair, making his way to the bar.

"Red wine at the minute" replied Robert "I'll stick with that, probably best."

Alistair filled their glasses and then sat with Robert on a plush green sofa, opposite where Max was slumped, snoring. Robert adopted the policy he felt most comfortable with in these situations, which was to get the first question in and let the other person do all the talking. "So what type of business did you and Thomas have, Alistair?" he asked, and then settled back against the arm of the chair and sipped at his wine.

"Mining. It's an area his family had entered into before Thomas was even born. Silver and Lead mostly. The Deacons had mined in Ireland for quite a number of years, but the Ballycorus site had been completely exhausted and they just used it as a base to smelt for other sites. In the end they shut it down in 1913, leaving them with just their Spanish and American sites running."

"Spain?" enquired Robert with surprise. "I didn't realise that. I met his father briefly before the war. He didn't look like he spent much time in Spain."

"He wouldn't have done then" Alistair continued. "But when they first opened it in the late 1800s I believe he spent a lot of his time out there, until Bernard was old enough to take over the reins. So Bernard ran the Spanish side at Sierra Morena, near Andalusia, from the early 1900s and once Thomas had finished school, to avoid having to enlist, his father sent him out to the Cerro Gordo site in the Inyo Mountains to take over the American side. It was there where he met Lilly, who was in California at the time."

"Blimey!" Robert exclaimed. "I didn't realise."

"Yes, unfortunately for poor Thomas the Silver production had peaked years before, it was mostly zinc by the time he got involved. The Spanish side was far more profitable at that stage."

"Makes sense" said Robert.

"What's that?" enquired Alistair.

"Oh nothing, just something that Lilly had said earlier about Bernard being better at the business than Thomas."

"I wouldn't say that's entirely fair. I mean if you just look at the balance sheets, sure, the Spanish site made more money for his Dad. But Bernard had far more help and advice from his father. He still went out there a fair bit, but he hadn't set foot in American since the turn of the century. Thomas had to work a lot harder."

"How come?" asked Robert.

Alistair sidled up closer to Robert and lowered his voice, despite the fact that the only other person in earshot was Max who was in no position to overhear their conversation. "Well let's just say his father had some other business he had to attend to in Spain" he replied, winking.

"Go on" said Robert, interested in uncovering more details.

"Well, and I don't know how true it was, but Thomas always claimed that his father had another woman out there. In Spain I mean."

"From what I understood he had women all over the place" said Robert.

"Oh yes, he did. Bit of a rogue he was. Once Thomas's mother passed he at least did the decent thing and married the governess that he had been having an affair with for some time. She's the mysteriously late guest that they were talking about earlier. But the only difference with his Spanish senorita is that she had a child by him. Again, he did the decent thing. He moved the child to England to be educated, and provided a house and an income for the mother in Spain. Hence his little jaunts over to Spain. His new wife didn't care; she was only interested in the money from all accounts."

"Hence Bernard's barb about her earlier" added Robert.

"Precisely" confirmed Alistair. "Thomas always played second fiddle to Bernard as far as his father was concerned. Not even marrying Lilly impressed him. And that's where I come in. Thomas and I knew each other as I had done some business with him in America. An opportunity came up to get involved in oil in the North Sea and we embarked on it. It's doing well too. Not that his father cared one jot about that either. He went to Spain to see him and tell him of his success but it ended in tragedy before he had the chance. The pair of them ended up squabbling at the entrance to one of one of the mine shafts. The quarrelling turned more physical and both men ended up falling to their deaths, their necks broken in the fall; terrible business."

"When was this?" replied Robert.

"About three months ago. It's tragic for the poor family."

"Hmmm…."

"What's wrong?" asked Alistair. "You look puzzled."

"Not puzzled as such," Robert replied, "I was just wondering who ends up with the family jewels? There's a lot of wealth attached to the Deacons. It seems quite messy."

"His father's last will and testament stated that everything was left to the boys and Sophia. It was a cause of great upset to Florence. She only got a nominal amount each year."

"Florence?" said Robert, his skin suddenly chilled by the realisation.

"Yes, their old governess who their father had married; Florence Deacon. A bit odd that's she's not here actually, I saw her in the dining cart on the way up here. Are you okay, Robert?" Alistair asked, noticing that Robert had a wide-eyed look of horror etched on his face. "Robert? Robert?" he repeated.

"Yes….yes I'm fine" he lied, trying to piece all the information together in his head. He had a sudden feeling of dread and felt sick to the pit of his stomach. Florence Deacon being murdered on the train and then Brannigan's suicide had seemed a horrible coincidence to Robert at the time, but now it was clear that the two things must have been inherently linked. But how remained unclear to him.

"Let me refill your glass, Robert."

"Yes," he replied. "Yes I could do with another one."

"That's the spirit. Unlike our friend here, who's definitely had enough" said Alistair, looking over to Max. "Jesus Christ! Robert, come here."

Robert went over towards Max who looked almost translucent. "I've never seen a man so drunk. He looks awful."

Alistair nudged Max and he roused slightly and made incoherent noises. "Where am I?" he muttered. "Who are you? Leave me alone, I….." he tailed off and drifted back into unconsciousness.

"We can't leave him here like this" said Alistair. "Let's take him to bed and let him sleep it off."

They each put one of his arms around their necks and hoisted him out of the chair, at which point Max, without waking simultaneously violently soiled himself and projectile vomited all over Robert's shoes and the bottom of his trousers.

"Christ almighty!" exclaimed Alistair. "Put him down again." They placed him back on to the chair and his head slumped sideways against his right shoulder. "He's unconscious. He didn't drink that much to be like this. This doesn't feel right. Be a good chap and fetch the doctor will you." But Robert was already on his way, leaving a trail of vomit with every step. He had torn up the stairs and along the landing towards the bedrooms before he realised that he did not have the first idea where the doctor was, so he started opening up all the bedroom doors and calling for the medic.

The first two rooms were empty, but by the time he went to the third Lilly appeared as Robert went to grab at the door handle. "What on earth is the matter?" she asked with a look of concern.

"It's Max, he's dreadfully ill. Where's Dr Hawthorne?" said Robert.

"Well his bedroom is there, but I have no idea if he's in there or not" Lilly replied, pointing to the room next to hers.

"That answers that then, I've already tried that room and it was empty" said Robert who rubbed at his forehead, unsure as to what to do next.

"Well let's go and find him then" said Lilly. "But if he's had one too many that's his look out."

"No it's not that, he's just made a terrible mess of himself and he's not conscious. And when he was he wasn't making any coherent sense."

Lilly looked down at Robert's shoes. "Oh I see what you mean."

"That's not the half of it!" he replied. "Come on, quick. We need to find him."

They raced down the stairs just as Dr Hawthorne was leaving the rear of the house that housed the kitchen and serving quarters. "Doctor, come quickly" Robert pleaded. "Max Kinkaid is exceptionally ill."

"Him too?" asked the doctor. "What are his symptoms?"

"He's a horrible ashen colour, he's vomited aggressively and soiled himself and was babbling incoherently."

"I see" replied the doctor with a concerned look on his face. "Take me to him at once."

Robert led them to the billiard room as swiftly as he could without slipping on the tiles due to the vomit on the soles of his shoes; Lilly and the doctor followed on with urgency. As Robert entered the room he froze to the spot. Max remained slumped in the chair but appeared to have vomited once more, all down his front and over his lap. Whilst Alistair, who had been left to try and wake him up, was laid face down over the billiard table; the back of his head had been staved in with a poker which lay on the floor and blood covered the green baize around his body.

"Oh my God! Robert you didn't say anything about Alistair!" screamed Lilly, whilst Doctor Hawthorne went over to examine him.

"But he was alive, when I left him. He was over there with Max. Who could have done this?"

"He's dead" confirmed Dr Hawthorne, who then made his way over to Max who was at least still alive, but continued to utter gibberish and appeared drowsy and unresponsive. "As I thought" uttered the doctor.

"What? What is it?" asked Lilly.

"I was informed that the chef felt unwell. Max has the same signs but far, far more acute. The chef should be fine, but there is nothing that can be done for Max. I'm afraid there is a murderer amongst us."

"You don't say" said Robert, pointing at Alistair's body.

"Naturally" replied the doctor." But I was not just referring to Mr Rashford. I'm afraid Mr Kinkaid has been murdered every bit as much."

"What do you mean?" asked Lilly, confused by his comment. "Max is still alive."

"For now he is, yes, but not for long, I'm afraid. Mr Kinkaid has been poisoned with lead."

Lilly gasped in horror. "But who would do such a thing?" She began weeping, then turned and ran from the room, across the hallway and up the stairs.

"And Mr Rashford was alive when you left him, you say?" asked the doctor.

"Yes" replied Robert. "I was only gone a couple of minutes."

"I see" the doctor replied, eyeing Robert plainly.

"What? Why are you looking at me like that? I liked the chap, I wouldn't have done this." The doctor did not respond. "Why are you just staring at me?"

"I believe we need to round up all of the other guests. Would you be so kind as to fetch them and meet me in the dining room, please" requested the doctor.

"Of course" said Robert, who began to make his way upstairs. Once again the first two rooms were empty; Robert cursed his stupidity as he remembered the doctor's room would naturally be so. As he approached Lilly's room, the door opened but rather than Lilly appearing it was Harold. "Miss Langham is needed in the dining room, Harold, as are you."

"I was just checking on Miss Langham, sir" said Harold in response. "She seemed most upset earlier at the news about Mr Rashford and Mr Kinkaid. What a most dreadful business."

"Quite" replied Robert. "Erm, Harold. I don't suppose I could borrow those clothes again could I?"

"Of course you can, sir. I'll fetch them right away."

"Thank you, Harold" replied Robert. The two men stood, neither one moving. Robert noticed that the scar on Harold's face had been covered up once more and whatever he had used to do so did not match his tanned skin colour exactly. In the light of the hallway and at close proximity it was far more obvious than it had been the previous night. "Erm, I just need to speak to Miss Langham, if you wouldn't mind, Harold."

"Of course, sir" said Harold, who reluctantly went on his way allowing Robert access to Lilly's room.

Robert entered and closed the door behind him. Lilly was sat at a dressing table with her back to him and appeared to be applying make up to her face. She had changed her clothes and was wearing a sleeveless dress with a dropped waist, sequin and bead embellishment to the waistband and a rounded neckline. He could see the top of her back which was uncovered to about four inches below the base of her neck which was entirely visible due to the style of her hair, being curled at the base of her blonde bob. His presence in the room alone with her would normally have made his stomach lurch with nerves, but the situation they were in supplanted any personal feelings he held towards her.

He coughed into his fist as if to announce to her his presence. "I'll be down in a moment, Robert. I'm just putting some make up on."

"Forgive me, Miss Langham, but I'm not sure anyone else will care about that at the moment."

She turned to face him and paused a moment. Robert could see that she had been crying and was covering up the damage. To his concern it also looked like she had a red mark on her cheek, roughly the size of a fist; his expression changed to one of concern for her.

"Call me Lilly, Robert. It's fine" she reassured him, perceptively. "I was becoming hysterical and Harold….." Robert looked incredulous with rage. "Really it's fine, Robert." She got up and walked towards him, pausing before him she smiled and kissed him on the forehead. "It's very sweet of you to be concerned though. But really, it's not necessary. Now if you'll hang on a second I'll round up the others with you."

She finished applying some henna and rouge as swiftly as she could and then turned to leave with Robert following behind her. "The doctor's downstairs and the room next to his is empty" Robert said.

"That's Bernard's room, where's he then?"

"I thought you may know?" Robert replied.

She stopped and looked at him earnestly, "do I detect a hint of jealousy, Robert?"

Robert blushed at her accusation, due to the fact that his question was tinged with a bitter tone. "Of course not" he lied. "But you two did leave together earlier…."

"Robert!" she gasped. "I'd rather die than sleep with Bernard."

"Don't say that" he said solemnly. "There's been enough death since yesterday and I don't want you to join the numbers."

"What do you mean since yesterday?" she asked with a look of panic on her face.

"Florence Deacon" he replied. "She was murdered on the train yesterday. I only realised who she was earlier when Alistair told me."

"Oh", she said, "Well that's terrible news, Robert; terrible. When will it all end, I wonder? Here, let's get Sophia" she said, opening the door to the Kinkaid's room. As they entered Sophia was sat bolt upright in the bed, rocking back and forth with a look of horror on her face. "Good God, Sophia" said Lilly. "Whatever's the matter? You're as white as a sheet. You look like you've seen a ghost."

Sophia fixed her eyes at the two of them stood in the doorway and stopped rocking, her mouth was open in shock and a tear slowly trickled down her cheek. "I have."

Chapter Fourteen

It had been several minutes since Sophia had spoken, but since then she had not uttered a single word of explanation as to what she had meant. Lilly had tried to extract from her what the matter was, whilst Robert looked on with a feeling of utter helplessness. Gone was the swagger and confidence that she had exuded in the dining room with him; replaced by sheer fear which seemed to grip at her very being.

"Robert this is no good" said Lilly. "You're going to have to go and fetch the doctor. I'm afraid she may need something stronger than brandy this time."

"Of course" he replied, but remained rooted to the spot, seemingly reluctant to leave them.

"Robert! Please hurry" insisted Lilly, prompting Robert to leave the room and go to find the doctor. As he tore down the stairs his mind was racing; 'who could have done such a thing? Max was reviled by everybody but what possible motive could anyone have to murder Alistair?' he thought to himself. He dashed into the dining room to find the doctor in discussion with Harold, their conversation broken by Robert's sudden entrance.

"Ah, Mr Johnson" Harold greeted him. "I've just laid out the suit on your bed, sir."

"Thank you, Harold. I'm afraid there's no time for that at the moment though. Doctor, would you please come quickly. Mrs Kinkaid is in quite a state and Miss Langham has requested that I fetch you immediately. I'm afraid everything else will have to wait until afterwards."

The doctor looked concerned at this news. "What is wrong with her, Mr Johnson?"

"I'm not entirely sure" Robert replied. "Shock I think."

"Ah I see" the doctor replied in a relieved manner. "That is not too much of a surprise given the circumstances of the day."

"It's not just that though, doctor. She seems quite gripped with fear as if in sheer dread of something. And she said something about seeing a ghost." The normally unruffled Harold reacted with a look of concern, whilst the doctor had a look of wry reticence which Robert was confused by. "What is it?" asked Robert.

"How ironic" Doctor Hawthorne replied. "Her husband passed away when you went upstairs to fetch her." The room fell silent. Max was a deeply unpopular man but his death was the third in the space of a few hours, and it had been a horrific death. "I will go and check on Mrs Kinkaid, Harold, Robert, would you be as kind as to move the bodies of Mr Kinkaid and Mr Rashford to Mrs Deacon's room please."

"Of course, Doctor" replied Harold. Robert did not reply; he was lost in thought but silently followed Harold out the dining room to complete the unpleasant task of moving the bodies.

"How are we going to do this then?" asked Harold. "One at a time between us would be best, I guess."

"Indeed" agreed Robert. "Let's move Alistair first."

"Makes sense" said Harold as they entered the billiard room. "He's the nearest".

"He's also not covered in vomit and shit" added Robert through gritted teeth as the strong stench of liquid faeces hit their noses.

"Christ almighty!" said Harold, wincing at the smell. "I see what you mean."

Robert picked up the head end of Alistair's body, concluding that blood from his head wound would not make any difference to his already ruined shirt. Harold carried him by the legs and between them they made their way up to Florence's bedroom. "Hang on a second" said Harold, as he struggled to open the bedroom door, nearly dropping the body in the process. "And we're in. Here, let's squeeze him on the bed right next to Mr Brannigan. That'll leave plenty of room for Mr Kinkaid on the other side, on account of the mess he's in."

"Good idea" agreed Robert, as they laid the body down next to Brannigan's and then made their way to get Max's corpse. "I'll leave the door open" added Robert. "It'll make it easier to get back in."

On their way down the stairs, Robert's inquisitive nature got the better of him. "I couldn't help but notice the scar on your face, Harold. It looked quite nasty. But it's disappeared today?"

"It was from the Somme" replied Harold. "I was with the 52nd Division and we were fighting with the Canadians. We'd been involved in heavy fighting and just seized control of an area at the west edge of the Hindenburg Line. There had been massive casualties on both sides, but we'd forced the Germans to retreat behind the Canal du Nord. The battle was won, but…."

"Go on" said Robert, eager to know more.

"But we were sent in for one last raid by our Captain. It was unnecessary. The enemy had withdrawn and had been defeated, but orders are orders. So forward we went and in the process a bomb went off about twenty yards in front of me, killing dozens of men. I was lucky; I just got a face full of shrapnel."

"I see" said Robert, respectfully. "And Captain Brannigan….."

"Yes" said Harold. "It was he who gave the orders, sir. He got himself in a lot of hot water that day with the top brass. He deserted the following day. We never saw hide or hair of him again, until he resurfaced after the war back in England. He was arrested and tried, but he had friends in high places and he was let off."

"God, I remember now. It was in all the papers. Caused quite a scandal I seem to remember" added Robert.

"That it did, sir. A lot of families lost loved ones that day, needlessly. The war was over not even two months later. A lot of men never got the chance to go home though, thanks to the Captain and his recklessness. So if you're thinking of mourning him, he's no loss."

"I see" said Robert. "Perhaps seeing you at dinner, and your face, perhaps he may have recognised you?"

"Perhaps, sir" replied Harold, stopping at the billiard room door and looking Robert unemotionally in the face.

"Perhaps the weight of it all was too much after all these years? Perhaps he was driven to take his own life as a result, maybe?" asked Robert.

"Perhaps he was" said Harold, entering the billiard room and bracing himself for the task ahead.

"But how come the scar only appeared at lunch yesterday and then disappeared again?" asked Robert, keen to pursue the matter.

Harold looked at him sincerely and said "I think I've said enough on the matter already, sir. If I choose to cover up my scar, that's my business, if I don't….well that's my business too isn't it? Brannigan shot himself. Now let it be."

Robert was clear from his response that he should desist from his questioning, but Brannigan's attendance had not been explained, and there were far too many unanswered questions relating to him; not least his connection with Florence. Her maid murdering her did not make sense to Robert at the time. 'What if Brannigan had murdered her,' he thought, then that may explain his suicide, but what if he did not? Either way there was still a murderer in the house; of that there was no doubt.

Turning his attention to the unpleasant task at hand, Harold had already grabbed the head end of Max, leaving the faeces-sodden trousers for Robert to handle. As they lifted, Robert could feel the moist cloth sliding over Max's calves and made him shudder at the thought of it. They carried him up the stairs and along the landing just as Lilly and the doctor were leaving Sophia's room.

"Oh for heaven's sake, who left that door open?" snapped Lilly.

"I did," said Robert, "to make it easier to get Max's body in there."

"Yes, and let the bloody cat in, no doubt!" replied Lilly.

As Harold and Robert entered the room with Max's body, Lilly was bent down picking the cat up from in front of the wardrobe. "Oh sorry" said Robert "I didn't think. How did you know it would be in here though?" he added as they laid Max's body on the bed.

"I didn't" said Lilly. "But there are dead bodies in here and the last thing we want is the cat getting at them is it?"

"Well luckily he seems obsessed with that wardrobe" Robert replied "I saw him scratching at it earlier....."

But Robert was cut off by a loud scream coming from Sophia's room, a manic, fearful noise which alerted the doctor to return to her room, quickly followed by the others. They were faced with the familiar site which Robert and Lilly had witnessed earlier. Sophia was sat upright on her bed with her knees up to her chin and her hands gripping her shins with a look of utter fear on her face

"Oh dear, she has had a relapse" Dr Hawthorne uttered. "Calm yourself my dear. Harold, fetch another brandy, please." Sophia shook her head and muttered something, "I can't hear you, my dear" said the doctor. She muttered again. "Speak up my dear, what is the matter?" he asked.

"DON'T GO IN THE WARDROBE!" she screamed.

Robert ran to the wardrobe with the others closely behind him. Ignoring the stench that had quickly filled the room, he pulled the wardrobe door open to reveal a body, laid in the foetal position, facing the back of the wardrobe and dressed only in underwear. "So that explains where Bernard had disappeared to" said Robert. Behind him stood Dr Hawthorne, Lilly and Harold; all of them silent, processing the discovery of yet another corpse. Sophia appeared in the doorway, shaking and crying.

"The cat was scratching at the door to get in" she sobbed. "I don't know why but I opened the door for it. It kept scratching at the wardrobe, so I looked inside and......"

She sobbed uncontrollably; the shock of finding her brother seemingly too much for the already emotionally fragile woman. Lilly put her arms around her and comforted her as Sophia sobbed against her shoulder. Robert looked back at the body then crouched down to inspect it more closely.

"What is it, Mr Johnson?" asked Dr Hawthorne.

Robert pulled something from the clenched right hand of the body and presented it in the palm of his hand to the others; some strands of blonde hair, about eight inches long and curled at the bottom.

"It wasn't me!" pleaded Lilly. "I'm being framed. Anybody could have taken those from the hairbrush in my room at any point today."

"Nobody has accused you" replied the doctor. "But it is clear" he continued "that one of us is a murderer."

"Why only one of us?" wailed Sophia, "it could be all of you. I'm not safe with any of you. Why does everybody keep dying?" She looked at the body of Max laid next to Alistair and Brannigan. "What happened to him?" she said coldly.

"He was poisoned, Mrs Kinkaid" replied Doctor Hawthorne. "I suspect with lead."

"How do you know this doctor?" asked Lilly.

"Because of his symptoms, Miss Langham" replied the doctor. "I have seen them before. I suspect that it was arsenic oxide; it is a water soluble solid which is tasteless and therefore a perfect poison to be added to someone's drink. In Mr Kinkaid's case, it could have been one of the many glasses of red wine that he had consumed before his death."

"But who would do such a thing?" asked Lilly, putting her arm on Sophia's to offer her support.

"I'm afraid that is something that I cannot answer, Miss Langham. All I can say is that it was the poison of choice many years ago, so common in Italy that it was dubbed 'Inheritance Powder'.

"It was you!" said Sophia suddenly, pointing at Robert.

"What?" he exclaimed. "Why on earth would I poison Max?"

"Because you wanted me to yourself" she replied. "You said so yourself, while you had me bent over the dining table."

"What?" Robert repeated. "No I didn't."

"Yes" she replied nodding at him. "Yes you did. You said you couldn't fuck me because of Max. So you poisoned him. I gave you the idea."

"What are you talking about?" pleaded Robert as the others stared at him with suspicion and, in the case of Lilly, disappointment.

"And you were the last person to be with Mr Rashford before he was killed" added Harold as Robert glared back at him, although unable to deny it.

"Yes" she continued. "I told you that Max added things to people's drinks and that gave you the idea. Oh I don't mind." She paused, switching from manic behaviour to a more calm and emotionless persona. She smiled at Robert and softened her voice towards him, "I think it's terribly romantic actually."

"Sophia…" Lilly uttered, concerned at her behaviour.

"Oh shut up, Lilly" she snapped. "You're just jealous. You've always been jealous. Anyway, that was your hair that Robert found in Thomas's hand."

"She's delirious" said Harold. "She doesn't even know which brother's which."

"Sophia, don't be silly" Lilly replied. "Are you okay?"

Sophia staggered slightly and appeared light-headed, once again staggering into Robert who caught her in his arms.

"Don't worry. That's just the effects of the sedative I gave her" the doctor said reassuring Lilly who had a look of concern that Sophia was coming to harm. "I intend to protect each and every one of us from whoever is committing these heinous acts. I suggest while we are still cut off by the storm that we lock ourselves in to our rooms until the morning. The storm will be over at some point soon and then we can summon the Police to take the matter into their hands."

"I agree" said Robert. "What about Sophia though? How can she lock herself in if she is sedated?"

"I'll stay with her" offered Lilly. "She'll be safe with me. No offence chaps but…."

"You're right" interrupted the doctor. "That seems the most appropriate course of action."

"And if she's dead tomorrow, we'll know you're not being framed" added Harold coldly, looking at Lilly who looked distinctly unimpressed with the comment but chose to ignore it.

"Right then," said the doctor, "I will bid you all a safe night. I suggest we meet in the dining room at eight am sharp."

Doctor Hawthorne left for his room, followed by Harold, whilst Robert carried Sophia once again to her bedroom with Lilly in close accompaniment. He laid her on the bed and swept her long blonde hair out of her face; she looked a picture of beautiful tranquillity, whilst all around her had descended into chaos and carnage.

"Thank you Robert, I'll get her undressed and make sure she's alright" said Lilly, who looked emotionally shattered.

"Are you okay?" asked Robert. "What I mean is, just look after yourself tonight won't you. Don't open the door to anyone, no matter what. Lock yourself in and look after the pair of you."

She smiled at him; her tired eyes still sparkling behind the multitude of other emotions that she was feeling. "Thank you, Robert" she uttered. "Make sure you follow your own advice though, eh. You can't be too careful." She took two steps towards him, took his arm in her hand and kissed him lightly on the lips. "You really are the sweetest man" she added. Robert half-smiled at her, almost embarrassed by what she had said.

"Goodnight, Lilly" he said, leaving the room and shutting the door behind him. He waited outside momentarily before he heard the sound of the door locking from the inside and then he made his way to his own room to lock himself in for the rest of the night.

Before doing so he went to the bathroom to wash his hands and face, although no amount of water and soap could remove the memory of handling Max's filthy corpse or poor Alistair's which had covered Robert's clothes in blood. On entering his room, Robert took his clothes off and threw them in the corner of the room; there seemed little point in trying to salvage them even if he wanted to. Harold was true to his word and had left the caramel coloured suit for him to use again; Robert placed it over the back of a chair leaving the bed completely free for him to climb into.

The sheets were cold to his skin when he first got in and he shuddered at the shock, having been used to the temperature of the room being warm from the heat of the fire. He pulled the covers up to under his chin and laid on his back staring at the ceiling. He cursed himself for ever coming to Knoydart in the first place. His status quo may have been drab and predictable, but at least it was safe. He gasped suddenly and jumped out of bed and raced to the door. He knew he had locked the door, he had consciously done so. But old habits die hard, and the compulsion to double check his previous actions compelled him to do so. A quick turn of the door handle confirmed what he already knew; the door was locked and he was safely ensconced within his bedroom until morning.

He got back into bed and repeated the process of tucking himself under his covers to get as warm as possible. His body and mind were tired but the adrenaline coursing through his body rendered him wide awake and positively unable to get to sleep. He was left alone with his thoughts which switched from one death to another and another and the burning question as to whose hand the victims had fallen to.

Robert's thoughts tumbled about in his head. Max had been poisoned by lead, the very product that the Deacon's mined. But then there was only Sophia and Lilly left from the family, neither of whom had anything to do with the business. And what of Bernard, squashed up in the wardrobe half naked; the circumstances defied logic? Max was clearly too weak to have killed Alistair, whilst Sophia could have slipped downstairs while Robert was searching for the doctor. But Sophia was the only one who had shown genuine remorse when Thomas's death was discussed and her reaction to finding Bernard's body was too fearful to be an act. In addition to that could a woman really have overpowered a man like Alistair; fit and strong and in the prime of his life, then bludgeoned him with such force? Robert was convinced otherwise, which likewise ruled Lilly out on the same premise. Also Lilly was in her room and then did not leave Robert's side until they found the doctor and then subsequently Alistair's body. The doctor had been downstairs at the time of the murder; he appeared from the rear of the house but then the murderer would have fled the scene somewhere. And Harold was nowhere to be seen either. Whoever the murderer was, Robert concluded, it had to be either Dr Hawthorne or Harold.

Robert could not think of a single motive that would drive the doctor to commit murder, but he was a quiet, enigmatic man who had given nothing away as to who he was or why he was there, other than the fact that he clearly knew who Harold was. Whilst Harold had displayed plenty of suspicious behaviour; the appearance of his scar which had been the catalyst towards Brannigan's death; he had served wine at the dinner and was best placed to poison it; how had he covered the scar up? Had he used Lilly's make up? He had free access to all of the rooms, had he taken hair from Lilly's brush to frame her? Poor Lilly; she had tried her hardest to ensure that her guests had a pleasant weekend and her efforts had ended in murder with her being lined up as the main suspect. Robert resolved that he would relay all of his suspicions and knowledge to the Police when they arrived in the morning, although he was not naïve enough to realise that he too would have to prove his innocence in all matters.

Robert's mind then turned to the arousal that he had felt towards Sophia earlier in the day. The Deacon name seemed synonymous with a poisoned chalice to whoever became involved with it; but Sophia transcended that. He thought of what she had said to him and he decided that despite her origins, he could indeed love that particular Deacon had the circumstances been different. But as he had been told the previous day; it was 'the wrong place and the wrong time.' She was undoubtedly beautiful and knew it, but she appeared scarred emotionally, no doubt from her unbearable existence with Max. Thankfully she was free of that particular emotional shackle now, but the scars of that as well as what she had endured in Knoydart would no doubt take time to heal. And despite how he had felt in the dining room, any feelings of lust towards her had been just that. Robert was clear in his mind that he would not take advantage of her vulnerability; she was too good a person for that. Moreover he would be forever a reminder of this fateful weekend where she had been entirely innocent, of that there was no doubt in Robert's mind.

Outside the rain continued but appeared much lighter than it had before, the sound of it only just audible above the ticking of the clock on his bedside table which had started to become almost hypnotic in its repetitive beat. As he listened to it his mind wandered from Sophia to Lilly, who was as innocent as Sophia and had endured as much but she had far more mental fortitude. She had come through the day and was still protecting Sophia and being strong for her sister-in-law despite the danger to her own life and the evidence pointing towards Harold or the doctor trying to frame her. The stark reality started to filter through Robert's mind. The famous Lily Langham, object of his affection from the age of thirteen and famous star of stage and screen, had kissed him. That fact put a smile on his face as he pictured her beautiful face and slipped slowly to sleep.

He heard a noise which made him open his eyes and he took a moment to decide whether he had been asleep or not. He did not remember dreaming but his thoughts seemed distant and therefore, he concluded, he had drifted off. He lay there silently wondering what had woken him up, when a light tapping came from the door. It had not been a dream, somebody was at his door; the tapping came again this time slightly louder. He quietly got out of bed and picked up the heavy iron poker from the fireplace and went towards the door, as the rapping came again, louder still.

Against his better judgement he turned the key to unlock the door, raising the poker above his shoulder and bracing himself to strike. He turned the handle and pulled the door open, then slowly lowered the poker down to his side. "I told you not to open the door" whispered Lilly.

"You did" he replied.

"So why have you?" she asked him.

"I don't know" he replied, absorbing her beauty. Robert rubbed his eyes, expecting her to disappear into a dream. But when he stopped she was still stood in front of him wearing the same dress as before and her hair and make-up were still in perfect condition, suggesting she had not yet been to bed. "Why are you here?" he asked.

"To keep you safe" she replied. She lifted her hand to show him a key. "Sophia is safe. I've locked her in."

"But…"

She put her finger against his lip to stop him speaking and threw the key to the floor, then went back to the door and locked them both in. She turned and slowly walked towards him whilst unfastening her dress; he stood in front of her in just his underwear in utter bewilderment. She stopped a foot from him and dropped her dress to the floor to reveal her perfect form before him.

"My God!" he uttered, transfixed by her beauty. She smiled with satisfaction, knowing the effect she was having on him and stepped towards him. She placed her index finger on the top of his chest and slowly ran it down towards his groin, making him shudder and his body arch backwards. Then she lightly pushed her finger against him with enough force to leave him lying on his back on the bed. Before he could sit up she had placed both of her knees around his waist and was removing his pants. She leant over him and kissed him passionately on the lips and then smiled with delight as she felt him throbbing against her left leg. She rose and walked towards the window. "What are you doing?" he asked her.

"You'll see" she said, looking over her shoulder towards him. "Lie on the pillows." He complied at once, his whole body wracked in tense anticipation. She took the curtain ties from each side of the window and returned to the bed, straddled him around his waist and began tying his wrists to the oak bedframe.

"What are you doing?" he asked, his mind panicking but his body over ruling his brain. She placed her finger on his lips again to quieten him. He was powerless to stop her; as captivated under her spell now as much as he was a child. She finished binding him tightly to the bedframe, the material cutting into his wrists painfully as she pulled them. She kissed him on the lips and slowly slid her body against his until she rubbed herself over him, making him moan with delight. She smiled again, enjoying the power and control she had over him. She opened her mouth wide and slowly dropped her head towards his groin; his eyes rolled back and his body shook slightly in gratification as she closed her lips around his penis and slowly moved her head up and down. The sensation to him was indescribable, not just because of her action, but because of the whole experience. It was almost too good to be true.

He began to throb inside her mouth; the pleasure intensified and his breathing started to turn in to a pant. She slowed the movement of her mouth and then gently pulled off him. "What are you doing? Why have you stopped? Please don't stop!" he pleaded, desperately. She stood up and looked at him, helpless and at her mercy, manacled to the bed. "What are you doing?" he repeated, confused and desperate at the same time.

She smiled a smile that he had never seen before and slowly started walking to the door. "Lilly, what are you doing" he asked, panic setting in as he realised there was nothing he could do to stop her.

She got to the door, turned and smiled at him. "You'll see" she answered and then unlocked the door.

Chapter Fifteen

His arm muscles tightened as he pulled and twisted them, but he was bound too tightly to the bed to make any difference. He looked at her in sheer panic; his body rigid in fearful anticipation and yet his voice utterly lost in the back of his throat. She opened the door fully and the light from the hallway immediately brightened the room, partly illuminating her in the doorway but making her facial expression clear to Robert. She looked assured, confident and single-minded in whatever she was doing, of which Robert was clueless. His chest began to betray his fear as it rose and fell sharply with each breath that he took. She could see the alarm from his eyes and body language and smirked in satisfaction. She stepped directly in the middle of the light, illuminating herself in front of him as he braced himself for something. He thought about screaming for help, briefly, but he remained mute and motionless, bewitched by what was being unveiled before him; completely under her spell. She stepped forward, flicked her dress out of the way with her right foot and then pulled a face akin to a startled innocent girl who had just happened to find Robert in the position he was in. She opened her mouth in mock horror and fluttered her eyelashes at him, then rose to her tip toes and began to almost flutter on the spot like a ballet dancer on pointe.

Robert watched, confused and yet beguiled by her as her foot movements slowly rotated her around away from Robert. She stopped and stood still before slowly and quietly uttering the words "You are my honey, honey suckle." She turned her head and when Robert looked at her face he realised what she was doing; she had adopted her stage face. She was performing for him. "I am the bee" she added, more spoken than sung and light enough for only him to hear. She wiggled her bottom at him, evoking memories of the first time that she had performed it. But unlike all those years ago, this time it *was* only for his eyes. She turned and walked slowly towards the bed. "I'd like to sip the honey sweet, from those red lips you see" she continued, staring intently into his eyes and winking at him. "I love you dearly, dearly…." she paused, as she climbed on to the bed and straddled his chest with her legs. "And I want you to love me" she continued as she gently slid up his chest towards his face, pausing over his neck and looking deep into his eyes. "You are my honey, honey suckle……I….am….the bee…."

She put both hands behind his head and her groin against his mouth and pulled the two together until he tasted her on his tongue. She rubbed herself against him slowly and groaned with pleasure, pulling his head tighter against herself with each movement of her body. He remembered the door being unlocked and wide open, of the potential danger of an intruder, of whether Lilly was responsible and whether he would be her next victim. He was powerless to resist her regardless of her ultimate intention but he did not care; if he was to die then what better way to do it. His penis, which had been rendered flaccid by the fear of her earlier behaviour, responded with animal instinct and became hard. His mind now focused solely on Lilly, who writhed in pleasure upon him. He flicked his tongue against her which changed her breathing to a pant and she squeezed his head between her slender thighs. He struggled to breathe, but in between gasps of breath he gorged on her, sucking at her desperately. She allowed him to feast on her before she pulled herself off him, leaving him panting and frantic beneath her, and then she lowered herself towards his waist. She did it slowly, teasing him, as he lurched towards her to kiss her but was prevented by the curtain ties.

She smiled at him with satisfaction, delighting in his desperation for her, and then slowly slid him inside her. They both groaned in unison at the sheer pleasure of it, as he slowly went deeper. Every urge he had wanted to be on top ravaging her, but he was powerless to influence anything; she was in complete control. She sensed his urgency and responded in completely the opposite way, slowing her movements to his frustration. He did not complain though, he submitted to her will as she knew he would. Neither of them had spoken a word, but she read his desires like a cheap book. She teased him by stopping her movements completely and at one point even lifting herself off him completely. She hovered over him and smirked smugly as he panted desperately for more, before satiating him by resuming her movements and then slowly increasing the speed. He could see the door wide open behind her. There had been no movement or interruption from anyone, but the possibility of it and the danger of it combined with her sexual teasing heightened his delight. She sensed it in the changes to his facial expressions which reflected his imminent climax and she responded in kind, almost at will. Their bodies combined in joyous ecstasy as he exploded inside her as she arched her back into a spasm of delight. He looked at her breasts, which were perfect and heaved with her short, sharp breath. He wanted to kiss them and touch them and then explore every inch of her, but he could not. She looked at him and smiled, then lifted herself from him and went to the door, which she closed and locked from the inside and then returned to the bed. She untied his hands and dropped the curtain ties on the floor before getting under the covers. He joined her and immediately embraced her, kissing her passionately and exploring her body with his hands, gently and softly.

He was relieved that he had trusted her and that he had not cried for help. He knew that she was not the murderer and he resolved to forget about what had happened and what lay before them the following day. Robert knew that this may be the only time he had with her, so he set about utilising that time to good effect. He wanted to please her again, so set about her entire body with his lips, his tongue and his fingertips until she was once again groaning with pleasure which in turn aroused him. To her delight he entered her again, this time from above her and he was in control, slowly and carefully probing inside her and kissing her gently. He was lost in her; utterly encapsulated with what was happening amidst feelings which transcended anything he had ever experienced before.

As he approached his climax, he pulled his mouth away from her lips and stared into her eyes, looking deep into her, conveying his feelings for her without words. She responded in kind, the two sharing a beautiful moment which culminated in a crescendo of ecstasy. He gently withdrew from her and laid gazing into her eyes. "I told you not to open the door" she said; the first words exchanged by either of them since her entrance.

"I'm glad I did" he replied, smiling. "That was quite a performance."

"You didn't do so bad yourself."

"I was referring to the song and dance routine. I think I preferred it naked to fully-clothed."

"Yeah, I bet you did." She stroked his face, his eyes suddenly showing signs of melancholy. "What's wrong?"

"That this isn't real. It's just a performance isn't it? Once tomorrow comes and goes, we'll all go back to our humdrum little lives. Well I will. And I'll never see you again. That's what's wrong."

She pondered his words, continuing to stroke his face, then stopping to cradle his head in her hand. "It doesn't have to be like that" she replied.

"Of course, the famous Lilly Langham, settling down in rented accommodation while I work at the local bottle factory." She chuckled. "See. Preposterous isn't it."

"If only you knew" she replied.

"Knew what?"

"Show me someone younger than thirty five who has the slightest idea who Lilly Langham is. Just because you know who I am and have put me up on a pedestal, doesn't make up for everyone else, you know."

"Rubbish" he countered. "Everyone knows who you are, or at least who you were."

"Oh thanks!" she said laughing. "What a flatterer you are."

"I didn't mean it like that. I mean….what I mean is…."

"Sssshhhh" she said softly, putting her finger on his lips. "I'm only teasing." He nibbled at the end of her finger making her squeal and giggle.

"Sssssshhhh yourself" he whispered. "You'll have Harold up here checking what's going on."

"Don't worry about him. He won't hear a thing" she said reassuringly and kissed Robert on the lips.

Robert pulled away suddenly. "What's with him anyway? It's like he's the boss of you sometimes, the way he speaks to you. I don't understand."

"Robert don't spoil it. You don't have to understand everything." She kissed him then laid her head back on the pillow and closed her eyes. "God I'm exhausted." Robert started to rub at the back of her neck with his right hand. "Oh God, yes, right there. Ahhh yes, don't move. That's perfect." He rubbed her for a few seconds more before her breathing turned heavier and she slipped into sleep.

Chapter Sixteen

She rested her head against his chest and stroked his cheek with her slender hand. For that moment the carnage of the previous forty eight hours had disappeared and the only distraction was the first birdsong of the morning, briefly offering hope of bright new things. His eyes had not moved from her for some time, even while she slept. His first thoughts upon her rousing were of her utter beauty, her fragility and how he wanted to protect her. At that moment he did not know whether he was protecting her from a malevolent force that had swept through the brief time they had spent with each other, or whether he was protecting her from herself. She rubbed her eyes with the back of her hand, smudging her eye make-up even more than it had been already. The pillow she had laid on was smeared with henna and rouge, whilst her hair was still perfectly curled on the left side but flattened slightly on the right where she had laid on it after succumbing to exhaustion.

This was the first time he had seen her in her natural state; without the bright lights, the perfect make up, the perfectly set blonde hair. To him she was even more beautiful because of it. She looked up to meet his gaze and smiled, exposing a flash of her teeth and the creases to the side of her eyes that had had barely three hours rest. He cradled her face and looked into her blue eyes. "I'd die for you," he said, his eyes fixed to hers.

"Why on earth would you want to do that?" she said, her voice croaking due to her dry mouth and her sparkle disappearing to be replaced with an expression more representative of the circumstances in which they found themselves.

"Because," he said, pausing to kiss her on the forehead, "some things are worth dying for."

"You shouldn't say things like that" said Lilly, frowning.

"I mean it. Last night when you…"

She smirked at him and his embarrassment. "Go on. When I was what?"

"Last night when you were…on me…."

"Yes…."

"When you tied me to the bed, I thought…."

"Go on" she said, encouraging him to continue despite knowing exactly what he was going to say. "What did you think?"

"I thought you were going to kill me" he said, smiling. "Silly isn't it."

"I know you did. That's why I did it."

"Why?" he asked.

"Why didn't I kill you? That's an odd thing to ask."

"No" he tutted, "why did you want me to think that?"

"Perhaps I was going to" she replied.

"And yet I'm still alive."

"You are" she said, smiling.

"You're not a very good killer then are you?" he replied, smiling back at her.

"Evidently not. I could have though, if I'd have wanted to."

"I know."

"You didn't stop me though did you?"

"I couldn't think of a nicer way to go" he said smiling. She leant over and kissed him then nestled her head against his chest as he lay on his back. She wrapped her left leg over his and squeezed him, whilst he cradled her head, lost in thought and staring across the room. Before long he could tell from Lilly's breathing that she had once again fallen to sleep, but his mind was too active to join her. His thoughts turned once again to the previous day and the terrible events that had occurred, then further back to the train journey where he lingered on the terrible sight of Florence's maid holding the bloody hairpin and of Florence herself. He remembered his initial entry into the carriage, Florence's haughty attitude towards him, the poor maid coyly averting her gaze in embarrassment, her brazen beau with the slicked back hair and then chills shot down his arms and legs as his eyes focused on the caramel jacket resting over a chair and he recalled the caramel coloured trousers of the fourth passenger in the carriage. He had been covered by his newspaper and was not seen again subsequently. It suddenly dawned on Robert that Florence's death and the deaths at Knoydart were far from coincidental. And then he remembered the man with the scar when he caught Betty on the platform. He had not registered before as his farewell to Betty had been the only focus at the time, but he realised where he recognised Harold from. It had been he who had looked at Robert when he called after Betty. He tried to remember what Harold had been wearing then but all he could see was his face and then Betty in her fawn dress. It was too coincidental, far too far-fetched to imagine the circumstances were unconnected. Harold had to be the murderer. He had killed Florence on the train and then got off early to avoid detection, making his way by another means. A car perhaps, Robert reasoned. That explains why he did not prepare her room; he knew she would never arrive to occupy it. Then his appearance at dinner had driven Brannigan to suicide. It was Harold who served the wine which poisoned Max, whilst he was unaccounted for at the time of Alistair's death. Bernard had been drinking heavily and would have been easy prey too, whilst he had clearly struck Lilly in the face, perhaps he had been interrupted before murdering her too. Thank God that he had interrupted him, Robert thought to himself.

  He stretched his arm to the bedside table and looked at the clock, which indicated that it was ten past six; nearly two hours before they were to reconvene downstairs. Robert fidgeted in bed, disturbing Lilly who turned over but then went straight back to sleep. Seizing the opportunity, Robert quietly stepped out of bed and put just the suit trousers and jacket on, picked up the poker, gently turned the key and then slipped out of the room. He quietly closed the door, reassured by the unbroken noise of Lilly's deep breathing and locked her in safely, putting the key in the inside pocket of the suit jacket.

  He quietly walked barefoot along the corridor, reasoning that Harold would be located somewhere in the servants' area towards the back of the house. He walked passed Sophia's room and was pleased to hear the faint sounds of her snoring safely in her bed. As he approached the end of the corridor by the top of the stairs he froze as it became clear one of the bedroom doors was ajar. Robert believed it to be Dr Hawthorne's who had been most insistent on everyone locking themselves in for their own safety, and yet his door was open. Robert raised the poker in readiness, unsure what or whom he might encounter. He slowly pushed the door open fully, arm at the ready to swing, muscles taught with stress. As the door swung open the sight before him filled him with horror; his heart pounded in his chest and panic filled his muddled head. Dr Hawthorne lay dead on the floor in his nightclothes, whilst Harold was laid on his back, naked, a pair of black knickers stuffed into his mouth, eyes filled with terror and hands firmly tied to the bed post with stockings.

    Robert approached him gingerly, just in case, but attempting to feel for a pulse indicated immediately that Harold was indeed dead. His bare skin revealed the extent of his injuries; substantial damage had been done to his chest, arms and upper legs. The damaged areas were bright red and raised and dappled as if hot candle wax had been melted on him and left to dry. They were at an extreme contrast to the tanned complexion of the rest of his body. He was cold to touch and his body, including his still erect penis, already showed signs of rigor mortis. This changed matters entirely and conclusively. He could not fathom why or how, but it was now clear that Lilly was in fact responsible for the deaths at Knoydart and she had also been on the train so most likely that of Florence's death too. She was the only person left in the house, Harold had met his death amidst the same bondage-based sex game that Lilly had played with Robert; yet he had survived. Their conversation resonated in his head;

    "You're not a very good killer then are you?"
    "Evidently not. I could have though, if I'd have wanted to."

    Robert felt sick to the pit of his stomach, he looked down at Dr Hawthorne, and a flesh wound on his head appeared to indicate how he met his death, the poker in his room which laid next to the hearth the most likely murder weapon. Robert looked in his right hand at the poker he held and strode defiantly back towards his own bedroom but stopped as he got to the door when he heard a muffled noise behind him. He spun around and raised the poker;

Harold's body remained tied to the bed, but the body of Dr Hawthorne slowly moved on the floor. Robert immediately rushed to his aid, dropping the poker and helping him to his feet. As the doctor rose he put his hand to his head and grimaced in pain.

"Sit on the bed" said Robert, leading him towards the bottom of the bed as far away from Harold's body as possible. The doctor sat and rubbed at the wound. "What happened?" asked Robert "Why did you open your door?"

"I heard a knock at the door; it woke me from my sleep. I don't know what time it was but I crept towards the door, picking up the poker on my way for protection and waited for another knock."

"Go on" said Robert, feeling a strange sense of déjà vu.

"A second knock came, so I whispered 'who's there? What do you want?' and then she replied 'I'm scared. Will you protect me?' So of course, I opened the door. I am a gentleman. I could not leave a lady unprotected with a murderer loose. What a silly fool I was" the doctor said, shaking his head.

"Then what happened?"

"I opened the door and Harold stood in front of me. I was taken by surprise; he grabbed the poker from me and struck me on the head. All I remember is hitting the ground and seeing him walk in followed by a woman."

"Lilly" Robert added, shaking with anger at how he had been duped by her.

"Oh no" said the doctor, "dear God what on earth?...."

The doctor had seen Harold's body tied to the bed for the first time, his mouth open in shock as he tried to process the sight. "Never mind that" said Robert. "What do you mean 'oh no'? Lilly is the only female here. Well other than Sophia but Lilly herself assured me that she had locked Sophia into her room from the outside and that she was safe. She's still in there now sleeping. I heard her and she had no way of leaving the room."

"Really? And when did she reassure you of this?" Robert did not answer but his look of shame told the doctor everything he needed to know. "I see" said the doctor.

"So it must be Lilly. She must have colluded with Harold, and then killed him herself to tidy up her loose ends, leaving…."

"Assuming me dead, just you, Mr Johnson" said Dr Hawthorne. "It is a possibility, yes."

"But there is no other explanation" replied Robert. "Like I said, Sophia is locked in her room with no means of escape, so it can't be her, can it?"

"Correct" confirmed the doctor.

"So it must be Lilly" concluded Robert.

"Not necessarily" mused the doctor.

"But" insisted Robert, almost high pitched in tone as he grew more perplexed, "she is the only other woman here. Correct?"

"Incorrect" replied the doctor, as Robert looked at him with wide-eyed incredulity. "You are forgetting the chef."

Robert looked dumfounded at Dr Hawthorne. "But….but…I thought…"

"That he was a man?" finished the doctor. "Then you would be incorrect. She most definitely is not. I examined her myself earlier on. That's where I was when you discovered Mr Rashford's body. She had complained of the same symptoms as Mr Kinkaid, but much milder. She will be fine in time. Fortunately for her, albeit…

"What?" asked Robert.

"Well" continued the doctor. "If what she was telling me was true, that is, and not a fabrication designed to mask her own involvement."

"Stay here and lock yourself in" said Robert, who picked up the poker and made his way downstairs to the kitchen. As he made his way to the stairs, he heard the sound of the door locking in Dr Hawthorne's room, whilst Sophia and Lilly were both safely locked in bedrooms. He trod each step as quietly and carefully as he could but with as much speed as he could muster without alerting anyone of his movements. He tried to ignore the portraits on the wall beside him, each one watching down on him with the same sneer of superiority until he reached the bottom where he felt an impulse to look at Thomas Deacon. The portrait was so real and life like it could have been him had he not fallen to his death three months earlier. Robert stared at his old nemesis for the last time before he heard the faint sounds of metal pots being moved in the kitchen at the rear of the house.

He moved with stealth from the hallway, through a door into a small dimly lit corridor with peeling paint and cardboard boxes stacked against the sides. Robert's senses were piqued and before moving on he stared intently at a coat hanging to his left with a pair of boots underneath it, poking at it with the poker to satisfy every ounce of doubt in his mind. As he moved his right foot forward the change from wooden floorboards to black and white tiles meant his foot made a clopping noise. His left foot made the same sound, resulting in him reverting to tip toes to edge closer to the door in front of him. The sounds within the kitchen had ceased, causing Robert to fear what might lie beyond the door, but he felt obliged to press on and find out the truth for once and for all.

He stopped at the door, gripped the poker firmly in his right hand and raised it to shoulder height for protection. With his left hand on the door-nob, he lingered for what seemed like an eternity, the only sound was the pulse he could feel throbbing in his head. Adrenaline coursed through his body and his breathing became rapid, his eyes fixed ahead at the door and his imagination rampant. He took a deep breath and slowly turned the nob which made creaking noises with each movement. He stopped and then with one swift movement turned it fully and pushed the door open and tip toed inside. Before him was everything one would expect to see in a busy kitchen; sausages lay individually on a tray on a large table central to the room, next to which was a large bowl of eggs. Scanning his eyes around the room Robert saw various kitchen implements hanging from the ceiling on long hooks, a large deep white sink, a stove which had a large pot of water that had reached boiling temperature and had steam rising from it as the water bubbled ferociously. Pots and pans lay in various states of use and a large rack of shining silver knives sat on the side counter with one very clearly missing from its slot. The other thing missing was the chef who had been there moments before, clanging about, alerting Robert to their presence.

The kitchen was a functional area with no place to hide, so Robert stepped toe by toe towards the back of the kitchen and beyond. The rear door was open and led to a further small corridor off which led to a back door and three rooms, all of which had their doors shut. The tiled floor ended at this door and was replaced by rough looking floorboards which at least afforded him the opportunity to walk normally. Robert could see that the back door was locked and stepped past it, slowly turning the handle of the first door he came to. The door was unlocked and Robert pushed it open without hesitation. Poker at the ready he stepped inside the small room which was lit by a candle that was not far from being burnt out. The room appeared empty but was instantly apparent that it had housed a man, from the clothes hanging from a hook on the back of the door and contents of the small bedside table. Robert examined it quickly; a razor set, comb, wallet and clock were joined by a small pot. He picked it up with his spare hand and examined it to no avail; it was label less with no obvious sign of its contents. He put the poker on the bed and opened the jar to find a smooth substance within; he rubbed some between his fingers and deduced that it was make-up. The room was obviously Harold's, but now Robert was clear that he had his own face camouflage, rather than having stolen Lilly's.

He returned the jar to where he found it, retrieved the poker and after that had a notional check under the fold-out bed, despite the fact that it was far too small to hide much more than a cat. He left the room without shutting the door to minimise any noise, and slowly turned the door-nob of the next room. Stepping into it swiftly, poker raised and ready to defend himself, he again saw instantly that the room was empty. This room had the same contents as the first, a small fold out bed which had been neatly made, clothes hanging from a hook and personal grooming items. This time the room obviously housed a female; a dress hanging limply on the back of the door, a small tumbler half filled with water on the bedside next to a brush with traces of brown hair. With nowhere to hide in the room, Robert again made the notional safety precaution of checking under the bed to satisfy his compulsion before bracing himself to enter the final room which he now knew housed the chef. He gripped the poker tightly and took a deep breath before creeping slowly and silently towards the open door. Just as he got to the doorway he stopped momentarily, his body instinctively telling him to push ahead but his mind screaming at him that something was not right. His compulsion to check and recheck drove him back into the room towards the bed, his peripheral vision having picked something out that was out of place.

    He crept back towards the bed, which was neatly made; blankets pulled up tightly and tucked in at the sides; single, uncomfortable-looking pillow fluffed up as much as it could be and placed neatly and centrally as if it had never been used. But there was a small lump at the near corner of the pillow that betrayed the otherwise impeccable nature of the bed. Robert pulled the corner of the pillow up and folded it back far enough to reveal what had been placed beneath it, just as the toilet flushed in the third and final room. His skin tingled and prickled and he dropped the poker to the floor which made a deafening sound to shatter the silence. The noise had alerted the chef and Robert heard the last door being unlocked and opened. "Who's there?" said a voice, measured and controlled. "I said who's there?" Robert did not answer and did not move. The poker remained by his feet and he stood frozen to the spot with his back to the open door. Footsteps started to make their way slowly from the third room towards where Robert stood, still frozen to the spot, staring at what lay beneath the pillow. It was facing upwards, creases betraying it's frequency of use and confirming to Robert who its owner was. The footsteps stopped in the doorway and still Robert remained motionless, staring down at a well-thumbed book; 'Murder in the Cathedral' by T S Eliot.

Chapter Seventeen

"For God's sake" said Betty. "What are you doing here? You scared the life out of me."

"What am I doing here?" asked Robert with incredulity at her comment. "That's rich. What are you doing here and why exactly have you got a knife in your hand?"

"Oh, sorry" she replied, lowering the knife which had initially been pointed at Robert. "I thought you were Harold."

Robert did not commit himself to answering that comment, choosing to remain as guarded as possible. He was crestfallen, torn between a woman he had been encapsulated with and a woman who stole his heart two days before; one of them being responsible for a series of horrific murders in conjunction with Harold. And Robert was in the unenviable position of not having the first idea as to which one was which.

"Why would you need a knife if I'd have been Harold?"

"Ugh" she muttered. "That creep; he makes my skin crawl. I had the misfortune of sharing a car with him from Carlisle. He seemed okay at first but last night he tried to ply me with wine. Quite insistent that I drink it, he was. So I pretended to just to get rid of him then spat it out when he'd gone, then poured the rest down the sink. I don't even like wine. Then he came into my room to try and have his wicked way with me last night. So I put my knee through him and pushed him out the door and locked myself in."

Robert mulled over her answer while she looked at him waiting for him to respond. "Hmmm. That would explain why you only had mild symptoms."

"What are you talking about? How do you know about that?"

"Dr Hawthorne told me" he replied, confusion etched on his face as he played through in his mind the different possibilities.

"Oh charming. What happened to patient confidentiality? Anyway he said it wasn't contagious so you and your friends have got nothing to worry about. You can enjoy your breakfast. Speaking of which if you wouldn't mind I need to be getting on with it." Silence ensued as Robert eyed her, while she waited awkwardly. "Robert?...."

"You have no idea do you?" he asked.

"No idea about what?"

"How many people are you cooking for this morning?"

"Well now you've graced us with your presence" she smirked "seven. Plus Harold and myself of course but we can eat later." Robert remained unmoved and unresponsive to her. "How was your curry by the way?"

"Astonishing. But that's not important right now" replied Robert, still working through the permutations in his mind.

"Oh, I see" said Betty, looking dejected. "Do you know what time I waited up till to get that ready for you?"

"You didn't have to" replied Robert as thoughts of Betty and Lilly flooded his brain, whirling around too quickly for him to process clearly.

"I couldn't bear to think of you hungry. Or thirsty" she said smirking. "Are you okay? Robert?"

"I think we need to go upstairs."

"I bet you do. Robert, you're serious aren't you? I can't, even if I wanted to. I've got to get breakfast ready. Plus Harold will be after me if I leave the kitchen. I'm under strict instructions not to. I went to yesterday afternoon when I heard that gun shot and he went berserk at me. Why were people shooting pheasants out of bedroom windows anyway?"

"You really don't know what's happened do you?" asked Robert. Betty looked at him confused, and he took the knife from her and led her by the hand through the kitchen to the main house.

"Robert, why are you bare-footed......and bare-chested?" asked Betty.

"It's a long story."

As they walked through the kitchen towards the door they heard footsteps approaching down the link corridor. Robert froze on the spot, let go of Betty's hand, pushing her behind him and raised the knife in front of his waist. Betty looked at Robert with concern, "Robert? What on earth is going on?" He remained unmoved as Lilly appeared through the kitchen door. She breezed in and greeted him immediately beaming her trademark smile, dressed in the attire she had so swiftly discarded only a few hours previously and hair and make-up impeccably restored to perfection.

"Ah there you are. I was wondering where you had got to! What on earth are you doing in the kitchen?"

"I could ask you the same thing" replied Robert, the knife held steady by his waist in his right hand, his left grabbing Betty's arm and keeping her behind him.

"Robert, darling, what's gotten into you? Why are you holding that knife and who on earth are you hiding behind you?"

Betty's eyebrows rose in surprise, "darling eh?"

"Oh it's the chef" replied Lilly, "how delightful. Shouldn't you be getting on with breakfast?"

"Well I was trying to but Robert here was trying to take me upstairs."

"Oh was he now? My, my! Robert darling, I can't help but feel a little disappointed and surprised, actually. Was I not enough for you?" Betty made a disgruntled grunt in disgust, but Robert ignored it, gripping her wrist tighter than before.

"That's enough" insisted Robert.

"I'm not sure it is, actually" replied Lilly. "I give myself to you last night and here I find you half naked with the chef and a knife in your hand. Forgive me but I can't help but feel a little put out. I mean she's supposed to be cooking you breakfast not going upstairs with you. And with me still upstairs warming your bed, or did you want her to join us? Because I doubt that's her style."

"I take that as a compliment" said Betty, leaning around Robert who continued to shield her.

"Yes you probably do, dear, don't you?" snapped Lilly, her tone suggesting more than just irritation.

"Enough" snapped Robert. "Leave her alone."

"I'm sorry darling, of course" purred Lilly, her perfect face snapping into place in its fixed position of delightful hostess. "I shouldn't speak that way to the staff, you're quite right."

"Staff now am I?" said Betty.

"Speaking of which" added Lilly "has anyone seen Harold. The table isn't even laid for breakfast yet and it's to be served soon. Oh well, he's probably tied up somewhere."

"That's not funny" said Robert, unmoved from the spot whilst Lilly swayed with her hands behind her back in a child-like way some five yards in front of them.

"What do you mean, darling?" asked Lilly, pouting. "Whatever's the matter?"

"How did you get out anyway?" asked Robert. "I'd locked you in."

"Silly you!" she replied "Did you think I wouldn't have a master key? I looked everywhere for you. Still I've found you now. Why don't we have breakfast in bed? She can bring it to us."

"No she can't" insisted Robert.

"Robert, really!" snapped Lilly. "I can overlook whatever it was that you were up to with Sophia." Betty scoffed sardonically. "But if you persist in defending this little slut then you'll offend me."

"That's enough!" barked Betty, pulling away from Robert and approaching Lilly. "I've put up with the vicious bile from your family for too long. I don't want to be part of your precious family, I never have done. I don't want your money, your land or your houses, not then, not now, not in the future. I earn my own money and if I'd have known that this job was for you, you two bit, washed up old whore, I would have turned it down flat. I knew it was too good to be true as soon as I heard how much it paid. But you don't get to talk down to me. Understand?"

It was Robert's turn to look perplexed now, as Betty glared at Lilly whose face wore an expression of faux horrification which quickly turned to sarcastic and patronising. "Where did they teach you language like that? Daddy wouldn't be happy would he, what a waste of an expensive education. Or was it your whore mother?"

Robert grabbed Betty and pulled her back before she could lunge at Lilly who smiled with saccharine sweetness at how she had unruffled Betty. "The Spanish really are a fiery race, aren't they? You really should learn to control yourself, Isabelita. Now get on with breakfast."

"Don't bother" said Robert. "Nobody wants breakfast."

"Don't worry" insisted Betty "I'd rather die than cook for her."

"Well" said Lilly, smiling "if you play your cards right…"

"What is that supposed to mean?" snapped Betty in response, the fact that Robert still held a knife in front of them suddenly being placed into a concerning new light.

"Oh didn't you know? I thought you were Daddy's clever little girl? Well it appears we have a murderer in the house. People have been poisoned and all sorts. Remind me again, who was cooking for us yesterday?"

"Ignore her" Robert interjected. "I know exactly who it is."

Lilly pulled the same mocked shocked expression as the night before when Robert was tied to the bed. The reminder of which angered him; he felt stupid at his weakness and the feelings he thought he had for her.

"You surely don't mean me, Robert, darling?" Lilly said, feigning hurt. "Surely you haven't forgotten the opportunity I had last night to kill you myself? Now why would I let you off if I was murdering everyone?"

"Robert, what's she talking about? Who is dead?" asked Betty.

"Well, firstly there was that common whore, Florence. She used to be governess to the Deacon children before she hopped into bed with your daddy. Then when the actual Mrs Deacon passed away it took her about five minutes to con the silly old sod into marrying her. A man of that age; I wonder what attracted her to the millionaire mining magnate….hmmmm….let me think about that for a second. Then there was Captain Brannigan. Poor thing; he ended up blowing his brains out after eating your curry. That was a tad harsh, I thought, it wasn't *that* bad! For an illegitimate whore, that is…."

This time Betty did not react at Lilly's barb, realising the gravitas of the situation and why Robert had the knife pointed in her direction.

"Where was I? Oh yes. Then there was Max; poisoned, according to Doctor Hawthorne. He ended up shitting his pants and dying on one of my chairs. I'll never get those stains out, never mind. Still no loss there, Sophia will be relieved at least, if she's still alive of course. Now was she alive when I went in there to do my make up? I can't remember now. Then of course there was poor Alistair, lovely chap but ever such a soft skull it seems; softer than the poker that smashed it to smithereens anyway. Lovely chap but a touch dull, especially in the bedroom. Then there was Bernard, dearest Bernard. Well he got so drunk he fell down the stairs and snapped his neck; should have taken more care I guess. Again, no great loss, an insufferable bore just like his brother."

"Bernard's not dead" insisted Betty.

"He is" confirmed Robert. "He's in the wardrobe upstairs."

"No he's not" insisted Betty. "He's out the back asleep in my toilet; he's been there since last night. He staggered through there last night, there was no point stopping him, he was too drunk to listen. He made it that far then fell asleep in the corner against the wall.

Lilly's face changed for the first time as the sound of footsteps came from the back of the kitchen and Bernard appeared clutching his head, fully clothed and most definitely alive.

"Bloody hell, my head" grimaced Bernard. "Is breakfast ready yet, Betty, old girl?"

"But if Bernard's alive then who is upstairs in the wardrobe?" asked Robert.

"You should know" said Lilly. "You're wearing his suit. The suit he wore on the train." Her right hand appeared from behind her back and she pointed Captain Brannigan's gun in the direction of Robert, Betty and Bernard.

"If only you'd have stayed upstairs Robert. You could have had it all; the inheritance and me. You still can if you want. But I don't think I can trust you. No, you've made it clear how you feel. Protecting that illegitimate Spanish whore rather than coming upstairs for breakfast with me. You are my honey, honey suckle. No, there really is no choice. I am the bee. The only choice remains who to deal with first."

"What the bloody hell?"

"I'll fill you in shortly" said Robert to Bernard, who had joined proceedings at the most unfortunate of times and stood dumfounded as Lilly tip toed theatrically from side to side, twirling the gun in her hand.

"Oh do fill us in Robert" said Lilly. "Fill us all in, why don't you. I like to sip the honey sweet from those red lips you see. Come on Robert, fill them in."

"Lilly and Harold have killed the rest of the guests" said Robert.

"Wrong!" sang Lilly, in an over the top falsetto tone.

"As well as Florence Deacon" added Robert.

"Hmmmm, closer but still wrong" Lilly replied.

"Lilly" Bernard pleaded "what the hell is going on, old girl. Am I still drunk?"

"Quite possibly, Bernard" replied Lilly. "But I must say I'm quite disappointed to see you alive still, albeit horrifically hung over. Harold was most insistent that he'd dealt with you. Hmmmm. He hated letting me down, he must have lied to keep me happy. He was always doing anything to keep me happy. That also must explain why you're still alive Isabelita. Most unco-operative of you not to drink your wine up like a good little girl" she sighed. "Anyway I hate to contradict you, Robert. But actually this was all Thomas's doing. He hatched a plan to fake his own death, bring you all here and settle a few old scores; after he'd killed his father, naturally."

"Bloody hell!" exclaimed Bernard.

"Bernard, please don't interrupt me. You know how I hate people upstaging me. Now where was I? Oh yes, so after pushing his father down the mine shaft, there was the little matter of the inheritance. Well to make sure he didn't get cut out of everything like he always was at the expense of Daddy's two favourites. Yes that's right, darling Bernard and his Spanish mistress's little whore. That's you Isabelita; just checking you were keeping up. So Florence, Bernard, Sophia and the aforementioned Spanish whore were to be murdered for the sole inheritance. Alistair's sad demise would ensure Thomas could have 100% of their business, while Robert…."

She paused and looked at him "Poor Robert. I did think that was slightly obsessive, trying to settle a score from when you were both at school, but he was most insistent. So with the plan hatched, silly Thomas entrusted me to hire a butler to, well, buttle, is that even a word? Anyway, I digress. Fortunately Daddy Deacon had paid for Isabelita to train in her dream job so finding a chef wasn't a problem, and Harold. Well, he's doted on me for years; poor thing. Ever since he failed as an actor, I mean he was good but who was going to hire him with that horrid scar on his face. Make up or not, I mean, he's hardly Clark Gable is he?

So with staff arranged, the only thing remained was to have Harold kill Thomas so that….oh…I guess I'd then inherit everything. How fortunate for little old me. I was quite peeved when Harold insisted on adding in Brannigan and Dr Hawthorne into the equation though. He had his own scores to settle, Brannigan for his unfortunate face and Hawthorne for keeping him alive and leaving him the disfigured mess he is today. Again, a tad harsh on poor old Dr Hawthorne, but there you go. Collateral damage, I'm afraid!"

"Jesus Christ!" exclaimed Bernard in genuine shock.

"Bernard, I warned you. Don't interrupt me" snapped Lilly, focusing the gun towards him.

"Steady, old girl. Steady. We can sort something out, don't worry."

"I said DON'T INTERRUPT ME!" snapped Lilly who pulled the trigger, firing into Bernard's shoulder.

"NO!" screamed Betty, as Robert held her around her waist to stop her from moving. Bernard fell backwards from the force of the bullet, hitting his head against a cupboard. He lay on the floor. Rolling and writhing in pain as Robert shielded Betty as tightly as he could.

"Oh do stop being so dramatic, Bernard. It barely hit you. Now where was I? Damn it Bernard, I've lost my train of thought. Anyway, you get the gist. Thomas was a bitter and twisted little bastard who murdered Florence to get the ball rolling. It was a spot of luck her maid managed to get herself arrested for that; a nice little bonus. The rest was all Harold. Well apart from Harold of course. I did that. And because of bloody Harold, it appears I also now need to dispose of Bernard and Isabelita because he wasn't man enough for the job. Jesus, if you want a job doing...."

"My name's Betty, not Isabelita."

"I beg your pardon. Are you blind or stupid? Did you not just notice what happened to brother Bernard?" said Lilly, her lip curling up in anger as she turned the gun towards Betty. Robert stepped in front of Betty to shield her as Bernard continued to suffer as blood seeped through his shirt onto the tiled floor. "Robert move out of the way."

"I can't do that" replied Robert. "Lilly put the gun down."

"And I can't do that. If you insist on protecting your little senorita, then I'm afraid I'll have to deal with you first. What a shame. I had such high hopes for us" said Lilly, as she pointed the gun at Robert's chest. "After all, you did say you'd die for me, didn't you? Well now you get to."

Chapter Eighteen

The impact was directly to the head and within a second the body hit the floor with a dull thud. Betty let out a whimper and began to weep uncontrollably; the shock suddenly hitting her. Bernard groaned in pain as footsteps slowly approached him. Crouching down to within a few inches from him, a hand reached out and inspected his wound with interest.

"You'll be fine, Mr Deacon. I'll find something suitable and sterilise it then I should be able to extract the bullet." Dr Hawthorne stood back up and placed the heavy copper saucepan on the preparation table next to the tray of raw sausages. "Betty, how are your symptoms?"

Betty rubbed the tears from her cheek and eyes as Robert squeezed her tightly. "Yes, much better thank you, doctor."

"Where did you find that saucepan?" asked Robert

"It was in the corridor on top of a cardboard box. It was the only thing I could think of to stop her. I heard a gunshot and thought I'd better come and assist in some way" the doctor replied.

"Just in the nick of time" said Robert. "Will she be okay?"

"She will, barring a headache and possibly a touch of concussion" said the doctor, looking over the unconscious Lilly who lay prostrate on the kitchen floor. "What we do with her now, I'm not so sure about."

"Well the weather is fine" Robert replied. "Harold's car is parked up outside. One of us can go and fetch the Police, while the others wait for their arrival and keep an eye on her. I have an idea of how to keep her secure."

Robert and Doctor Hawthorne carried Lilly up the stairs and into Robert's bedroom. Laying her with her head against the pillows, Robert picked up the curtain ties and secured her by the wrist to the bed frame the same way she had secured him the night before but in very different circumstances. Once secure he gazed at her; eyes firmly shut and her breathing soft and steady. She had been responsible for orchestrated butchery, yet looked at this moment the very picture of beautiful serenity. Robert briefly imagined her waking, preparing herself for her day and playing host once more around the breakfast table. He could not help but feel sad at the beautiful tragic contradiction that lay before him.

"Do not linger on any thoughts of regret or guilt, Mr Johnson" the doctor said, interrupting Robert's stream of consciousness. "You were not to know of the evil that lay beneath the beauty on the outside. Choose to save your pity for those who fell because of her."

"Hmmm" replied Robert reticently.

"You do not agree?"

"It's not that. Absolutely they deserve our pity. It's just" he paused. "It's just, she seemed so…."

"Perfect?"

"Precisely; things aren't always what they seem."

"If someone is too good to be true, they probably are, Mr Johnson. It makes me thankful and appreciative for what I have."

"I know exactly what you mean" agreed Robert.

"I'll make my way to find the Police now, Mr Johnson, and alert them to this dreadful business"

"Do you know where you're going?"

"I do not, but there's a public house not far from here, The Old Forge I believe it's called. I'll head there initially and get directions from the landlord and return post-haste."

Robert nodded and the doctor smiled politely, nodding back in recognition, and then made his way at pace from the room and down the stairs. Robert could not bear to look at Lilly any longer and made his way to the window. Leaning against the window ledge and looking at the view, he squinted slightly as the bright sunshine dazzled him. From left to right as far as the eye could see was beautiful landscape, thick with densely growing trees and fields full of fauna. Although separated from it by glass, he breathed in deeply, inhaling nothing but the stale air from the bedroom, but imagining himself reborn by the sight and sounds before him.

Doctor Hawthorne appeared on the path below him and made his way across the gravel towards Harold's car, every footstep causing a satisfying crunching sound until he reached the vehicle. Within moments the car pulled away, cautiously at first as the doctor negotiated the controls as well as several large concrete plant pots in between the house and the end of the driveway. Whilst he had been watching the doctor's departure, Robert's mind had not deviated from one thought and one thought alone. The words of the elderly lady on the train niggled away at him and compelled him to act upon them. He had missed opportunities before, he had also attempted to take them and been dashed in the process. That mattered not now, he reasoned to himself; fortune favours the bold. At that moment he heard Betty ascending the stairs and making her way to Sophia's room; he steadied himself and began to focus his thoughts towards her.

Betty unlocked Sophia's room to find her sat on the back of the bed, hunched against the headboard, with a fearful look on her shattered face. "Betty? Is that you? Oh Betty, how lovely to see you. Please be careful won't you. Horrible things are happening. Horrible, horrible things."

"It's okay, Sophia" Betty reassured her. "It's all over. Come here" she added, cuddling her and kissing her on her cheek. "It's all over."

Robert appeared in Sophia's doorway, pleased to see her safe and well. "Oh hello Robert, it's so lovely to see you."

"Good morning, Sophia. Are you feeling better?"

"Oh I'm much better, thank you, Robert. I'm dreadfully sorry about last night. I don't know what got into me. Betty, I'm afraid I made a dreadful fool of myself."

"Sophia, it's fine" Robert said reassuringly. "Don't think any more of it; the wrong place and the wrong time. That's all" he added looking ruefully at Betty.

"That's very sweet of you, Robert. Betty, Robert was ever so gentlemanly. How very sweet. I dread to think what most men would have done in the same circumstances."

"Hmmm" said Betty. "I'm glad to hear it."

"Sophia, do you mind if I borrow Betty for a minute? Actually no don't worry" said Robert, realising her need was greater than his.

"No please" she replied. "I'm fine, honestly. Betty you go."

"No that's fine" said Betty. "I'll stay here and look after you. I'm sure whatever Robert wants to say can wait until later."

"Absolutely" agreed Robert. "I'll leave you to it."

"Unless…."

Betty paused as Robert hung upon her every word. "Unless of course you just say what you're going to say right now. Go on, Sophia won't mind" said Betty, enjoying watching Robert squirm before her.

"Fine" said Robert, resolutely, taking Betty as well as himself by surprise. "Betty, Isabelita, whatever your name is, whoever you are. I've been floating along for years, wasting my life and waiting for someone like you to come along. I'd given up waiting; presuming that you weren't out there and I was destined to be alone. But along you came, when I least expected you to. You woke me up. You ignited the fire in me. I love your complexion, your olive skin, your beautiful dark hair. I love your intelligence, your passion, your clothes and your love of food, your obsession with that God forsaken book. I love the creases on your nose when you giggle. I love how you sip at water instead of wine. I love you. I love you, Betty. I love you. If this the wrong time, I'll wait. If this is the wrong place….what am I thinking, this is definitely the wrong place….we'll go somewhere else, anywhere else, by train. I'll reserve a table in the dining cart. I thought I'd lost you, otherwise I never would have…."

"Stop" said Betty. Sophia sat there beaming, while Betty stood and walked over to him, leant up on tiptoes and kissed him on the forehead. "It's definitely the wrong place. It's also not the best time, if you think long and hard about it. Is it?" Robert smiled and shook his head. "But" she added, pausing to prolong his agony. "Why don't you take me out for lunch sometime? How does that sound?"

"That sounds perfect" replied Robert, smiling broadly. "Just like you."

Disclaimer

This is a work of fiction. Names, characters, businesses, places, events, locales and incidents are either the products of the author's imagination or are real but used in a fictitious manner. Any resemblance to actual persons, living or dead, or actual events is purely coincidental.

Or to be more specific....

All characters are imaginary apart from the ones portrayed in both the Music Hall section as well as in the Hollywood section, with the exception of Lilly Langham who is fictitious. Whilst the music hall characters were all real, their appearance on the bill the night that Robert watches them was manufactured. I merely selected an array of acts who were all appearing in that particular era, they may not have performed at the same time and location together. Needless to say, because Lilly is fictitious, she obviously did not steal Marie Lloyd's act on that fateful night, and there is no suggestion that Lloyd was upstaged in such a way by anyone else. In much the same way that although the Roscoe Fatty Arbuckle section is based on a real life event, Lilly was obviously not present at the time and The Cincinatti Kid was a fictitious film for the sake of the plot of this book.